Desert Song

Angela Dorsey

Desert Song

Original title: Horse Angel #2 – Desert Song
Cover and inside illustration: Jennifer Bell
Cover layout: Stabenfeldt AS
Published by PonyClub, Stabenfeldt AS
Edited by Kathryn Cole
Printing: GGP Media, Germany 2004

ISBN: 82-591-1149-7

The sun is hot above me. I cannot see it but I can feel its glory on my skin. Where am I this time? Where have I been sent? I feel her call to me. Aria. She is near.

The first time I shift to a new place always takes all my energy. I am blind for too long. Weak for too long. I know the Great One is protecting me, keeping me safe from harm, but it is hard to wait to become strong. I sense Aria's fear and long to go to her. Soon. Soon. I must be patient.

Ah, now my eyesight is returning. And now I can move my fingers. Dry dirt and sand are beneath me. Am I in the desert? Yes. The broad expanses spread away, sage and sand shimmering in waves of heat. And, to one side, rugged red bluffs climb to the azure sky: foothills and canyons with arid mountains behind.

Where is Aria? I cannot see her, but I sense her near. Soon I will be at her side.

DESERT VISTA JUNIOR HIGH

INFORMATION BULLETIN

From the Desk of Principal Lybbert

**To all Students of
Desert Vista Junior High School**

You have no doubt heard of the unfortunate accident that occurred this morning when a car struck Sophie Taylor as she crossed the street to enter the school grounds. The dark blue car then sped away. The police have since apprehended the driver of the vehicle.

We have just received word that Sophie has a broken arm as well as many cuts and bruises. She will be out of school for the remainder of the week and I'm sure she will appreciate any wishes from her fellow students for a speedy recovery.

Please remember to be cautious in crossing the streets at all times. Obviously, not all drivers obey the laws and you should not suffer the consequences of their reckless actions and disregard. Above all, be safe!

Principal Sally Lybbert

Sophie put down the book she was pretending to read when her foster parents walked into her hospital room. They had been talking to the doctor in the hallway and, though Sophie tried hard to hear what they said, she hadn't heard anything more than differently-pitched murmurs.

"Hey there, Sport," said Joel, Sophie's foster dad. "How're you feeling?"

"Okay," said Sophie, though really she wasn't. Her arm throbbed and the rest of her muscles were becoming sorer and sorer as the hours passed. The doctor had given her pills to help with the pain, but they weren't working yet.

"You want to sign my cast?" Sophie tried to sound cheerful as she held her right arm out toward her foster dad. She hoped he wouldn't notice her eyes flinch in pain or the expression on her face tighten.

"I'll hold it steady," offered Kalene, Sophie's foster mom. She sat on the chair beside Sophie, put her hands under the cast and held it firmly.

"You don't have to," said Sophie. "I can do it."

"I know you can," said Kalene. "But I want to. It's my favorite thing to do in the whole world: hold my daughter's cast."

Sophie couldn't stop flinching this time, but the pain she felt wasn't physical pain. It was an ache in her heart. Kalene had called Sophie her daughter, again. She had done it a few times over the last two months, and every time she did,

Sophie was reminded that she wasn't really their daughter. She was just a foster kid. Someone that no one wanted for a daughter. The government paid Joel and Kalene to feed and clothe and take care of her, and Sophie knew that one day Child Services would come along for no reason at all, and tell her it was time for a new foster home. She knew because it had already happened too many times.

But this time I wish it were different, thought Sophie. *I never loved living in the other places like I love living with Kalene and Joel. I've never felt so much like I was home.*

"It does hurt, doesn't it, Sport?" asked Joel, when he noticed the sadness in Sophie's large gray-blue eyes. "I wish I could take the hurt away."

"I'm okay, really," said Sophie, trying to make her voice sound tougher than normal. She lowered her cast. *Kalene and Joel will really want to get rid of me if they think I'm a wimp,* she thought. *The last thing they want is a pouting, whining baby for a foster kid.* "It doesn't hurt that much," she added in a brusque voice.

Joel and Kalene glanced at each other and then Kalene looked back at Sophie. "The doctor wants you to stay in the hospital, Sophie," she said. "He thinks you're fine, but he wants to keep an eye on you overnight, just in case there are problems."

"What problems? I feel fine. I can't stay here. Really I can't," said Sophie. She knew her voice sounded too panicky and forced herself to sound calmer. The next words were more controlled, but still urgent. "I have to go home tonight. I have to."

"It'll only be for one night," said Joel. "We'll be here early tomorrow morning to take you home."

"But what about Twixie?" asked Sophie, suddenly thinking of Joel and Kalene's big black and tan mixed-breed dog.

"She'll miss me. I play with her every night. She'll think I'm neglecting her!"

Joel laughed. "Trust you to think of the dog's feelings above your own health, Sophie," he said. "Believe me, we'll *all* miss you. But we'd rather have you here in the hospital just for the one night."

"Twixie will survive," added Kalene. She smiled at Sophie but her voice was firm. "It's important that you stay."

"But…" Sophie started again, but then she fell silent. The familiar breathless feeling of being unable to speak swarmed over her, just as it had countless times when she was younger. Just as it had even a few months ago, before she had started to feel comfortable around Joel and Kalene. She tried to force her uncooperative mouth and tongue to form words but couldn't do it.

"Sophie, you were hit by a car," Kalene said kindly. "The doctor thinks there's nothing more than the broken arm, but he, and we too, don't want to take any chances. You are black and blue and you're scraped up. Just in case the doctor missed something, we want the nurses to check on you during the night to make sure you're okay."

"But you can check on me at home," said Sophie, finally finding her voice, even though it sounded small and hopeless.

"Yes, but we're not professionals," said Kalene. "We won't be able to tell if there is something else wrong until you're very sick. Now there's no point in arguing. You *have* to stay."

Sophie didn't reply. How could she tell them that she had to get home to take care of Aria? How could she tell them that the Arabian mare they thought was stolen months ago, was hungrily waiting for her in a hidden corral deep inside one of the willow-choked canyons? Sophie pictured the beautiful gray mare stomping her hooves and watching the trail to the corral, impatient for Sophie to come with her hay and grain. She would wait until long after dark. When Sophie didn't come – couldn't come – Aria would be frightened. She would feel abandoned.

More than anything, Sophie couldn't stand the thought of Aria feeling abandoned. She knew how awful it was to wait for someone to return, to wait and wait and wait for days. To believe that any second they were going to come back because you knew they loved you and would never leave you. Not *really* leave you. To convince yourself that they went out to buy some bread, because you were so hungry. She knew what it was like to promise yourself and God and the angels you hoped were watching – but most of all your mom who wasn't there anymore – that you would be good if she just came home. You wouldn't make noise and you wouldn't cry and you wouldn't ask for ice cream, let alone bread. Sophie knew what it was like to wait, believing that the next second her mom would open the door, that she would walk into the room and smile and say everything was going to be different now. And then to have her never come. The thought of Aria alone with fear like that, even for one night, was too terrible to contemplate. "But…" Sophie tried one more time, brushing her long, brown hair away from her face.

"No more 'buts'," said Joel and Kalene together, their voices firm, and Sophie knew there was no point in arguing anymore. She had no choice. Aria would have to wait.

When darkness fell, the mountain lion crept from the shallow den he'd found in the rocks. He raised his head high and sniffed the air. When he couldn't smell the hunters he leapt from one boulder to the next, smoothly and steadily climbing to the top of the precipice. His paws slipped once on the rocks and dry pebbles bounced and tumbled downward, their rattle echoing off the canyon walls. The big cat didn't stop to look down. He surged to the top of the bluff.

The lion stared in all directions, stopping to sniff for foreign smells. The hunters weren't there. Could he have lost them? They had tracked him for days, the hunters and their dogs. In trying to escape, the mountain lion had traveled far from his home. Then a thunderstorm had hit the mountains and they began to close in on him. Rather than holing up and waiting for the storm to pass, the lion sensed that this was his chance to escape. He ran through the storm, terrified of the lightning and thunder that crashed and boomed around him.

Now, for the first time in days, the lion felt safe. He could kill freely again. Not that he was hungry. The lion had killed a young calf the day before and eaten a portion of his prey before the dogs came too close. But he wanted to kill again. He needed to kill again. He yearned to see the death-horror in his victim's eyes and longed to feel warm blood soaking his paws. He purred

11

softly to himself remembering his last victim and the satisfaction he'd felt when the calf's bawl faded to silence.

The lion stiffened. He smelled something very near. It was the same smell as another of his recent kills: a horse owned by hunters. It was a large, dark brown animal with flowing black mane and tail. He killed it quickly one night while the hunters slept, before they could wake and stop him. Then the lion had skulked away unharmed into the night, leaving behind shouts of rage.

Like dark ooze, the mountain lion slipped along the ridge top, silent and deadly. Within a few minutes he was looking down at a single gray horse, trapped in a canyon. The mountain lion dropped into a crouch and slunk toward the horse. All his senses were in tune. He heard the mare's impatient step as she paced the enclosure. He saw the moon on her gleaming side. He smelled her frustration.

Suddenly the gray mare sensed him. Her huge frightened eyes stared into the shadows that held him. The lion didn't slow. He knew she was trapped. The mare's fear washed over him, making him growl with pleasure. Her terror only made him more eager for the kill.

Where is she? I can feel her before me, but this looks like another canyon choked with willow bushes. Could Aria be trapped inside?

Wait! A narrow trail cuts through the willows. There are deer tracks but no horse hoof prints. Yet the trail looks worn as if more than deer have used it often. I will follow.

The trail dead-ends in a fence of willow branches woven tightly together. It is ingeniously built and very effective. Aria would not be able to get through, yet to humans who may chance this way, the fence and gate look like thickly matted willow; nothing more. Here is a small hole in the bottom of the woven twig gate. No horse could fit through, but a person could. A small adult. Or a child.

Aria. There you are! My beautiful Aria, glowing silver like the moon, your coat as soft as downy feathers. Why are you here? Who penned you in this forgotten canyon and then left you here, hungry and alone? And why?

You are so frightened. I can sense what you fear as well. There is a terrible danger here, though I cannot tell yet what form it takes.

Do not worry, my beautiful one. I will stay with you. I will keep you safe.

The cat saw IT. He stopped abruptly and lowered his belly to the ground. His quiet growl turned vicious as he watched the Bright Creature move to stand beside the mare. For a moment, he wondered if he could bring it down. He knew the mare would offer little assistance, if any, to the creature. But then the Bright Creature turned toward him, its eyes searching the shadows.

Slowly, the mountain lion backed away. He could tell the Bright Creature was not human, though it took a human form. Its voice, speaking softly to the mare, made the cat cringe and the gentle light around it terrified him beyond anything he had ever seen before. Pain pulsed through his dark heart as he looked at it, yet he was afraid to pull his eyes away. He fought his desire to whimper, forced himself to creep slowly backward, farther and farther from the Bright Creature. Finally, the mountain lion felt he was far enough away. Like a ghost, he turned and disappeared.

Safely out of sight beyond the ridge top, the big cat broke into a silent run. Within minutes he was more than a mile away. Finally, he stopped and shook his head, trying to remove the image of the Bright Creature from his mind.

Filled with sudden rage, he sent a piercing scream catapulting into the quiet night. He glared back the way he had come with narrowed eyes and growled, a low sound full of hatred, then slunk away, searching for a easier victim.

Sophie's sleep was interrupted all night. Every few hours the nurse came into her room and took her blood pressure, listened to her heart and read her temperature. Sophie had never felt so cared for – or so irritated. It was hard enough to fall asleep when her entire body felt like wild horses had trampled her. Her arm throbbed and her right side, bruised and battered from the car's impact, ached terribly. She found some relief lying on her left side, although it too, was covered in bruises and scrapes from when she had struck the road after bouncing off the hood of the car. Sophie shifted and turned painfully trying to get comfortable. Finally, she accepted there was no position she could lie in that didn't hurt. She lay on her back, stared up at the ceiling and forced her mind away from her discomfort.

But without her pain to focus on, thoughts of Aria in danger popped into her mind. *What if there is a brush fire in the canyon and Aria is trapped inside the willow fence? What if she escapes and steps into a hole as she gallops away and falls and breaks a leg? What if she gets lost and just disappears into the desert and I never see her again? Or what if she tries to squeeze through the crevice and gets stuck?*

But Sophie kept coming back to the worst thought, the one that was most likely to happen. *What if Aria starts to have her foal and there are complications?* Sophie knew the Arabian mare had never foaled before. What if the foal or even Aria died? Sophie would never forgive herself if that happened. More than anything, she wished Aria could be safe in her stable at home, with the veterinarian just a phone call away. But that was impossible. Kalene and Joel could never know of the foal's existence. Never.

Finally, Sophie drifted into a light, restless sleep. Visions of gray Arabian mares trotted through her dreams; some called to her for help, some neighed in greeting, and some whinnied in pain and confusion. All of them wanted her to come. All were impatiently waiting for her, needing her.

At 6:30 a.m., the nurse came into the room again. She smiled at Sophie with an overly cheerful smile. "And how are you today?" she asked brightly.

Sophie groaned and pulled the blanket over her head.

The nurse chattered on as if Sophie had answered, pulled the covers back, took her vital signs again, then told her the doctor would be in soon.

"Are my foster parents here yet?" Sophie asked the nurse.

"Not yet, dear," said the nurse. "Visiting hours aren't until eight o'clock."

"But they're not coming to visit. They're taking me home today," insisted Sophie, suddenly frightened she might have to stay another day. *I better start acting healthier. And be more cheerful,* she decided and sat up in the bed.

"I feel fine. See?" she said to the nurse. Sophie slid off the edge of the bed. She gasped in pain when her feet hit the floor. Every muscle in her body was protesting. "See? I feel great," she said in an unconvincing voice.

"Now you get back into bed," ordered the nurse. "The doctor will be here soon and he's the one you need to impress. There's no point in putting on an act for me."

Slowly, Sophie climbed back in. "I'm just stiff and sore, that's all," she said to the nurse.

The nurse smiled at her again. "I know," she said, then added "Would you like some more painkillers?"

"Yes, please," said Sophie.

About 20 minutes after Sophie had swallowed the pills she began to feel better. Then her breakfast came and she spent the next hour pushing the mushy oatmeal around her bowl and staring out the window. The day looked bright and hot, even though it was still early morning. *Thank goodness Aria has water,* thought Sophie. *Otherwise I would have to tell Kalene and Joel about her. She would die without water in this heat.*

When the doctor finally came, he took only a few seconds to examine Sophie's chart. Then he asked her how she felt.

"Fine," said Sophie quickly. "I feel fine. Just a little sore is all."

"You can go home with your parents when they get here," the doctor said. "I'll ask the nurse to tell them you need to come and see me next week so I can have another look at that arm, okay?"

"Okay," agreed Sophie. She didn't mind going to visit the doctor. She just didn't want to stay in the hospital.

"And you take it easy for a few days. Lie around and watch lots of videos," commanded the doctor. "No school for the rest of the week, either."

Sophie smiled for the first time. "Really? Awesome!"

"What's so awesome?" came Kalene's voice from the doorway. Joel entered the room behind her. As the doctor discussed Sophie's condition with them, Sophie slipped from beneath her covers and grabbed her clothes from the locker beside the bed. She carried them with one hand as she stepped painfully toward the bathroom.

"Wait, Sophie," said Kalene. "Here are some clean clothes." She took Sophie's ripped and dirty ones from her and handed her a duffle bag. Within a couple of minutes, Sophie was almost dressed. The hardest thing to put on was

18

her shirt. She was glad Kalene had packed her biggest, baggiest T-shirt in the duffle bag but even so, she had trouble fitting her cast through the sleeve. When she came out of the bathroom, the doctor was gone. Kalene and Joel were sitting on chairs beside her bed, waiting for her.

"I'll brush your hair for you and pull it back into a ponytail," offered Kalene and opened her purse. She pulled out a hairbrush and began to search for a hair tie. "You won't be able to do it yourself for a while."

"Is it okay if we just go?" asked Sophie. She grimaced. "I just want to get out of here."

"You betcha," said Joel and rose to his feet. "Your hair looks great anyway. And we have everything all ready for you."

"What do you mean?" asked Sophie, suddenly nervous. "What do you have ready for me?" Joel was always coming up with crazy ideas.

"Your transportation, of course," said Joel. He pointed to the door leading out into the hallway. A wheelchair sat just outside the door.

"Alright!" said Sophie. "Can I really? They'll let me?" She was already moving toward the wheelchair. "Can I do some wheelies?"

"Not with a broken arm, you can't," said Kalene firmly. "Joel will push you out."

The ride in the wheelchair was just as much fun as if Sophie had been allowed to do wheelies. Joel raced her up and down a few empty corridors, narrowly avoiding detection by the hospital staff. Joel and Kalene knew many of the people in the hospital. They would screech to a stop to talk to some of the older patients for a few moments, then they would be off again, the patients waving to Sophie as she disappeared down the hallway.

Sophie, Joel, and Kalene had almost finished the rounds

of the entire hospital when they spun around a corner and almost hit a nurse. The tray she was carrying went flying. Joel and Kalene hurried forward to help her pick up the silver implements scattered across the floor. They apologized as they helped the nurse put the tools back on the tray.

When they were finished, all three of them stood. Sophie, sitting in the wheelchair, thought how funny Joel and Kalene looked standing before the nurse, almost like kids that had done something bad at school. The nurse's mouth was a tight red line across her face.

"I remember the day you were born, Joel James," she said in a sharp voice. "I had to stay up all night trying to keep you alive. You were trouble then, you are trouble now."

"Sorry, Nurse Morgan," said Joel and hung his head. He glanced sideways at Sophie and winked.

"And who is this young lady you are spiriting away from us?" asked Nurse Morgan.

"This is Sophie, our foster daughter," said Joel. "She has a broken arm."

"I can see her arm is broken, Joel," said Nurse Morgan. Her eyes, large behind their glasses, examined Sophie from head to toe. "You're one lucky little lady, Sophia. Things could have been much worse for you."

"I know," said Sophie in a squeaky voice. She almost couldn't say anything, but somehow she forced the words out. She breathed an inaudible sigh of relief when Nurse Morgan turned on Kalene.

"I can see it's already too late for you, " said Nurse Morgan, focusing her attention to Sophie's foster mom. "Joel has already gotten you involved in too many of his escapades, but you should think about the bad example you are both setting for Sophia. Racing down hospital corridors. It's disgraceful!"

"Yes, Nurse Morgan," agreed Kalene. Then Nurse Morgan was gone, striding purposefully down the hallway with her tray balanced before her. Sophie was sure it wouldn't dare fall again.

"The only reason I didn't die when I was a baby was because I was too afraid to," whispered Joel.

"She's amazing," said Sophie. "Scary, but amazing."

Kalene laughed. "She's like a flash flood. Once she's swept on by, things are never the same again."

Joel spun Sophie's wheelchair around and they made their way as sedately as possible to the front entrance. Joel left Kalene and Sophie to get the truck, so he could pick them up at the door.

"The doctor said I didn't have to go to school for the rest of the week," Sophie said to Kalene.

"I know. We already phoned the school and asked for some homework for you. Good thing you didn't break your left arm since you're left handed," replied Kalene. She smiled when Sophie groaned at the thought of homework. "Max is coming over today after school to visit for a while, too," added Kalene. "I told her she could babysit you when we go out tonight."

"You're going out?" asked Sophie, trying to keep the hope out of her voice. It would be so much easier to take Aria her food when Joel and Kalene were out, so much easier than having to sneak out after they went to bed like she usually did.

"We're not sure yet. We'll wait and see how you feel first, okay? We bought those tickets to the play, remember? But we don't have to go. I wouldn't mind spending a quiet night at home either."

"But you bought those tickets months ago," said Sophie, surprised. She knew Kalene in particular, had been looking

21

forward to going to the play. "You can't stay home. I'll be fine, especially if Max comes over. You and Joel should go."

"Well, we'll see how you feel tonight," said Kalene. "I would like to go, but if you need me, I'd much rather be home." She looked down at Sophie's sceptical expression and laughed. "Really, I would," she said. "You're much more important than a night out on the town."

"I'll be okay," Sophie insisted. "You guys go. And I don't need a babysitter either, even though Max is probably the funnest one I could think of." She smiled as she thought of her best friend, Max. She was always doing things she shouldn't, and then acting so surprised when she got caught. And she *always* got caught. "I'll be tired anyway," Sophie added. "I hardly got any sleep last night. The nurse kept bugging me. And Twixie's good enough company."

"If you still feel okay about us going by tonight, then we'll go to the play," said Kalene and put her hand on Sophie's shoulder. "But I still want Max to come over. I don't want to leave you alone. Even if you count Twixie as company, she can't phone anyone if there's a problem."

"Okay. It'll be fun," Sophie forced herself to say. Though her voice was calm, her thoughts were in turmoil. *Should I tell Max about Aria? I don't want to wait until late to go to the canyon when Aria's going to be so hungry. And maybe Max can even help. I know I can trust her not to tell anyone. But she can't act too guilty either, or they'll know something's wrong.*

When Joel's truck stopped in front of them, Sophie climbed slowly into the front seat and Kalene got in after her. As they drove away from the hospital, Sophie's thoughts continued.

Really it's good that Max is so bad at lying. It means

22

she's a good person. Not like me. But she doesn't have much to lose either. If Joel and Kalene find out about Aria, they'll send me away. And if I have to leave, I don't know if I could stand it. Even if I don't deserve them.

No one has come all day. Has Aria been abandoned by whomever brought her here? I could take her home, I know she could lead me there, but the Great One says no. The one who brought her here must be the one to take her home. I do not know why but I believe it is true. The Great One knows all. I must keep Aria safe and well cared for until someone comes. And if her foal is born, I must help them both.

Aria was so frightened when I came. No, more than frightened, much more... she was terrified. What made her feel that way? It still puzzles me. I could sense a presence when I first arrived in the canyon, though I could not tell what it was. The energy it left behind, in the air, in the wind, and water, is not that of a normal being, neither man nor beast. It is something far, far scarier: something twisted and malformed in spirit. It contains a great evil that seeks the death of others – that seeks horror.

Aria thinks I am protecting her and perhaps I am, by just being here. By waiting, waiting, waiting at her side. Waiting for further direction from the Great One. Waiting for someone to come.

But this I know: I am not enough to stop an evil such as this. I do not have the power.

The phone rang just as Joel and Kalene were about to leave. Sophie groaned inwardly. More delays! But Kalene only talked on the phone for a minute before she hung up. "That was Allen and Trish," she said to Joel, who was standing at the door waiting for her. "They were wondering what was taking us so long. They've been ready for hours apparently."

"Did you tell them we'd already be gone if they hadn't phoned?" asked Joel.

"No," said Kalene, flashing an exasperated look at him. "Because it isn't true." Kalene reached out and gave Sophie one more hug. "You're *sure* you don't mind us leaving you tonight?" asked Kalene.

"We don't mind if you want us to stay," added Joel.

Sophie smiled. She could tell that Joel wasn't as excited about going to the play as Kalene was. "You just want to get out of going," she teased him, then she added, "No, really. I want you to go. Max is here and I'll call you if I need you to come home early."

"All right, but remember Max's mom is just a few minutes away," Kalene said. "You remember the number?"

"Don't worry, Mrs. Branson," said Max from behind Sophie. "I remember the phone number."

"Of course you do," laughed Kalene.

"Come on, honey," said Joel. "We're going to be late. Allen and Trish are going to start hitchhiking if we don't get there soon."

25

"And you remember our cell phone number?" Kalene asked Sophie as she moved toward the door.

"Yes. And I have it written down, too." Sophie smiled her most reassuring smile at Kalene. "Don't worry. I'll be fine. Max and I are just going to watch a movie and eat the popcorn you made us."

"Well, you two have fun," said Joel as he herded Kalene out the door, then turned to press his foot against Twixie's chest so she couldn't follow them.

"Have fun!" the girls called as the door shut behind them. Twixie stood beside it and whined for a moment, then trailed after Sophie to the living room.

Max collapsed on the couch with a huff of exasperation. Her short black hair swung around her head like a fringe as she shook her head. "Your mom is major paranoid," she said to Sophie.

"Kalene's great," said Sophie, as she scratched Twixie's back. "I've never had anyone worry about me before. Not like that, anyway. It's awesome."

"Well, I'm glad you like it," said Max, arching an eyebrow. "It would drive me nuts."

"Too late. You're already nuts," countered Sophie and pulled her long hair behind her head with her hand. "Help me with this, will you?" she asked Max. "I need to braid it and I can't do it myself."

"Why do you need to braid your hair?" asked Max, rising from the couch. "We're just going to watch a movie."

Sophie took a deep breath. "I've got something to tell you, Max," she said, her tone serious as she looked into the dark eyes of her friend. "But before I do, you have to promise you won't say anything to anyone. Ever. You can't even act guilty."

"I can't tell anyone why you're putting your hair in a braid?" asked Max as she pulled Sophie's hair back and

26

divided it into three pieces. "You make it sound so serious." She laughed, then fell silent when Sophie didn't laugh with her. "You're not joking, are you?" she asked when the braid was finished and Sophie turned toward her.

"No," answered Sophie. "And I'm only telling you because I have to. I need your help. No one else knows and no one can ever, ever find out."

Max paused for a moment and looked into Sophie's eyes, her expression puzzled. "Okay, I promise," she finally said.

"Are they gone for sure?" Sophie asked as she hurried to the window. They had taken Kalene's car. Only Joel's truck stood in front of the house. Sophie turned back to Max.

"I'll tell you quickly, then I've got to go," she said to her friend.

"What? You can't go anywhere. You have a broken arm," said Max, her eyes wide. "Where're you going?"

"I'll tell you everything, but I have to start at the beginning, okay?" said Sophie as she sat on the couch. Max sat beside her. "It happened last spring, a few months after I got here," started Sophie, her left fingers picking at her cast. "Joel and Kalene let me ride Aria because she was the only horse they had that wasn't in foal or didn't have a foal at side, and I can't ride Rolly. He's too, well, he's a stallion and they knew I couldn't handle him."

"So what happened?" asked Max.

"We were out on the desert one day. It was really hot and I got off to let Aria rest in the shade. Anyway, I did something so stupid! I fell asleep."

"Oh no," breathed Max. "And when you woke up, I'll bet Aria was gone. But that doesn't make sense. She didn't disappear until a few months ago."

"But, you're right. She was gone when I woke up," said Sophie. "But it was even worse than that. She was with the wild horses. They didn't know I was sleeping in the shade of the canyon and they weren't very far away. When they spotted me they ran, but Aria turned back when I called her. I was so lucky. I never took any more chances with her, but then…" Sophie took a deep breath as Max patiently waited. "Then, late in the fall, Kalene said something about Aria getting fat. They cut back on her feed a bit, but she just kept getting bigger. That's when I realized she was in foal."

"She was in foal to the wild stallion?" asked Max.

"Yes," said Sophie. "He's pretty cool, but he's not an Arabian and now the best, most expensive mare Kalene and Joel own is in foal to him."

"But what's wrong with that?" asked Max in a puzzled voice.

Sophie sighed. "The foal will hardly be worth anything at all, and Joel and Kalene are having such a hard time with money. They borrowed money to buy Aria, and Kalene works at the library because the farm doesn't make enough yet. If it never does, they'll have to sell everything, including the horses, to pay their debts. Aria's foals should be worth thousands of dollars, not just a few hundred."

"You sure know how to get in trouble, Sophie," said Max, shaking her head. "This is worse than anything I ever did."

"Don't rub it in," said Sophie, rolling her eyes.

"So what happened next?"

"I couldn't let Kalene and Joel find out what I'd done. They'd be sure to send me away," said Sophie. "So I decided to borrow Aria for a while."

"What? You mean that Aria is still around here somewhere?" asked Max, incredulously.

"Yes," admitted Sophie. "I made a corral for her in one of the willow canyons back in the foothills and then, one night, I took her there. I tried to make it look like she had been

29

stolen, and that's what Joel and Kalene and the police think. No one suspects me at all. Joel and Kalene were even worried about *me* when Aria went missing. They kept telling me they would find her and bring her home."

"So you've been sneaking out there to take care of her," concluded Max.

"And that's why I had to tell you. I have to go to her now. She hasn't eaten since before my accident. You've got to cover for me. Kalene is probably going to phone a few times during the night to see if I'm okay. You've got to stay here and watch the movie and answer the phone and tell her I'm sleeping." She paused when she saw the doubtful look on Max's face. "Please, Max? I promise I won't call you Maxine anymore."

"Of course, I'll help," Max said. "I just hope they believe me."

"It'll be easier over the phone," said Sophie. "They won't be able to see your face. You won't have to look anyone in the eye."

"Okay," said Max. "But I have one more question. What does all this have to do with me braiding your hair?"

"So it doesn't get so much hay stuck in it," said Sophie, smiling as she stood. "It's hard to brush my hair with a broken arm. I might have to cut it short like yours."

"I'll help you get the hay ready for her," Max said, following Sophie toward the front door. "Kalene won't phone this soon. They're probably just picking up their friends now."

"Thanks," said Sophie. "Really. I couldn't do this without you."

"Hey, no prob. That's what friends are for," replied Max with a grin. "It'll be fun. I just wish I could go with you."

"Me too," said Sophie and wondered why she hadn't told Max about Aria before.

The two girls pulled on their shoes and boots and within seconds they were out of the house, walking toward the closer of the two small barns. The green irrigated fields beside the buildings glowed in the pink sunset. Sophie couldn't stop herself from slowly turning in a complete circle. The house and the barns, the sunset-washed fields with the desert stretched behind, and the distant mountains all looked like a scene from a fairytale. Sophie drew in a deep breath and slowly exhaled. It was so glorious. Living in the desert still gave her that funny feeling in her stomach as if butterflies were fluttering their wings against her insides.

"Isn't it wonderful, Max?" she asked her friend, who had stopped and was looking at her strangely.

"Yeah, I guess," Max said.

"You just don't see it the way it is because you've lived here your whole life," replied Sophie. "I remember the first time I came to the ranch. I was so amazed. It was like something out of a movie."

"Speaking of movies, when you get back, remind me to tell you what it was about in case Kalene and Joel ask you," said Max.

"You're always so practical," said Sophie. She laughed and started walking again. "It's a good idea though, even if I'm supposed to be sleeping through it."

"Hey Soph, you still haven't told me everything," said Max, as Sophie struggled with the barn door open and fumbled for the light switch. "What are you going to do with Aria? You can't just leave her up the canyon forever."

"I'm waiting until the foal is born and old enough to wean. When it's a few months old, I'm going to turn it out with the wild horses. It can go live with its sire's herd, and then I'm going to bring Aria home. I haven't decided what I'm going to tell Kalene and Joel yet. Maybe that I found her walking down the road toward home. I read a book once about a horse that was stolen, but managed to return to its old barn."

"That sounds pretty suspicious to me. I don't know if they'll believe it," said Max, sceptically. "Especially if Aria's healthy. She won't look as if she's traveled a long way by herself."

"Maybe you can help me come up with a different plan," said Sophie as she found the switch and light flooded the barn. Eager neighs greeted them. "We have a few months to think of something. The foal's not even born yet."

"When is it due?" asked Max.

"Any time now," answered Sophie.

When Sophie and Max walked into the barn most of the horses left their feed to watch over their stall doors. Sophie had learned to love them all, even the grumpy white mare that lived in the end stall on the right. Rosie had been the last to warm up to Sophie, but now, even she was looking over the door in anticipation. Her two-week-old filly was trying to do the same. Sophie could see Starlet's dark nose poking over the wood, but the filly was too short to see over.

"Just a minute, Starlet," called Sophie. "I'll be right there."

As the girls passed the first stall, a dark bay stallion thrust his sculpted head over the stall door. A loud neigh pierced the air.

32

"Hey, Rolly, old boy," Sophie said as she turned toward him. "How are you doing tonight? Did you miss me?"

Rolly was the herd sire and, other than Aria, was the most beautiful horse Sophie had seen in her life. He had won scores of ribbons in important shows and the second barn on the property held eight mares that belonged to people who were paying to have their mares bred to him. Their owners were all hoping for the next National Champion foal.

Just like we are, thought Sophie. *Kalene and Joel had such high hopes for Aria and Rolly's future foals. I wish the baby she's about to have could have been Rolly's, instead of the wild stallion's. But Aria and Rolly can have a foal next year. I know their baby will be the most beautiful foal in the world.*

"I know you miss her, Rolly, but don't worry. She'll be back in a few months and I'll take good care of her until then." Sophie reached out to stroke his nose. The stallion lowered his powerful head and snuffled in her hair, blowing strands across her face. Sophie laughed and pushed her hair out of her eyes.

"He sure is beautiful," said Max softly beside her. "Almost too beautiful to be real."

"I know," said Sophie. "Kalene says that if Rolly knew how gorgeous he was, he wouldn't pay any attention to us lowly humans."

"Yeah, he'd be way too good for us," said Max.

Sophie leaned forward and kissed the stallion on his lowered forehead, right in the middle of his white star. "And you're a pest too, aren't you boy? A very big pest. And much too hard to handle under saddle. I wish I were good enough to ride you out to Aria's canyon with the hay and grain tonight."

"Hey, how *are* you going to get the hay and grain out to

33

her?" asked Max. "You can't ride your bike with a broken arm."

"I'm going to have to walk and pack it," groaned Sophie.

"Do you want me to go instead? That way you can answer the phone yourself when your mom calls," said Max.

"I wish you could, but you don't know the way. I hid Aria so no one would ever find her. You could be wandering out there for days and not see any trace of her," said Sophie. "But it's going to be awful. My arm aches already. And the rest of me is so sore."

"What if you rode one of the other horses?" asked Max.

"They're all due to foal soon or have babies that would have to tag along," said Sophie. "I can't take the chance of something happening to another one of Kalene and Joel's horses."

"I wish I could do more to help," said Max, her voice discouraged. She ran her hand through her short black hair.

"Me too," agreed Sophie. "But you're already doing lots. If it wasn't for you, I'd have to wait until Joel and Kalene got home and went to sleep, then sneak out and hope they wouldn't get up in the night to check on me. This way I can go a lot earlier and have it all done by the time they get home."

Together the two girls walked along the line of stalls. As they passed the next stall, Sophie averted her eyes. The sight of Aria's stall standing empty made her feel guilty. Kalene and Joel still hadn't moved another horse into it, even though both barns were full and they could use the room.

Max and Sophie stopped at each of the two stalls after Aria's and spent a few seconds with each mare. Max admired a new foal she hadn't yet seen, then they crossed the barn aisle and greeted the horses on the other side.

When they reached Rosie and Starlet's stall, Max gasped.

"She's getting even cuter. Every day she's prettier. So tiny and perfect," she breathed and reached over the door. "Can I take her home yet?" The dark gray filly whinnied to Max, then reached out and sniffed at her hand.

Sophie laughed. "It would be great if your mom and dad let you have a horse, especially when you guys have some land and an old barn already."

"Maybe some day, but it could never be Starlet," said Max, her voice sad. "She'll cost a lot more than my parents can afford. But she'll be here for a while. I'll just spend lots of time with her while I can." She reached as far as she could toward Starlet. The little filly didn't move away and Max scratched her neck. Starlet curled her lip at Max and the girls giggled. Then Rosie moved in front of her baby and gently pushed Starlet back.

"Sorry Rosie," said Sophie. "I know it's time for her to go to bed." She patted the white mare on her shoulder.

"I'm going to come visit again though," Max said to the white mare. "You'll get to like me eventually, Rosie, or my name isn't Maximillian."

"It isn't Maximillian," said Sophie with a laugh. "It's Maxine."

"Shhh! She doesn't know that," replied Max. "And besides, you promised you wouldn't call me Maxine any more."

"But I didn't say I would *start* calling you Maximillian," said Sophie and rolled her eyes at Max. "You've got serious name issues."

"I just don't know why my parents didn't call me Megan or Samantha or Heather. You know, a normal girl's name," replied Max.

"Maxine is a normal name," said Sophie as the two girls turned toward the end of the barn where the hay was stored.

35

"Correction – *was* a normal name," said Max. "I don't think anyone but me has been named Maxine in the last hundred years."

"Well, it's unique, anyway," said Sophie. "You've got to look on the bright side."

Max's only reply was a huff. When they reached the haystack, Sophie held out the net and Max stuffed fresh-smelling hay into it. As soon as the net was full, Sophie scooped some sweet feed mix into one of the buckets. Then she sprinkled some special horse vitamins on top of the feed and stirred. She slipped her good arm under the bucket handle, letting it hang from the crook in her elbow, and swung the hay net over her good shoulder.

"I can help carry it for a little way," said Max, and held her hand out.

"Okay," agreed Sophie. "I just wanted to be sure I could carry both." She swung the hay net off her shoulder and Max picked it up.

Rolly and the mares watched Sophie and Max longingly as the two girls walked back through the barn. Their liquid brown eyes were fixed on the bucket.

"You guys already had yours," said Max as she reached for the light switch and pulled the door shut behind them. "Stop begging."

Sophie and Max walked into the field behind the house. The sunset was fading. At the back of the pasture, Sophie laid the bucket on the ground and climbed through the fence. Then Max passed the grain and the hay net over to Sophie.

"Be careful, Soph," said Max. "I know you've been doing this for months, but it wasn't with a broken arm before."

"Don't worry," said Sophie reassuringly, picking up the bucket and hay. "I'll be fine. And I'll do my best to be back

36

in three hours. Joel and Kalene will probably be four hours at least, but I don't want to take any chances."

"I wish I could go with you," said Max.

"Me too," said Sophie. She smiled at Max before she turned away. "See you soon." Then her eyes moved to the hills in front of her and she started to walk. Sophie prayed that Aria was still in her canyon, deep in the pink-washed hills, then she quickened her pace.

I'm not going to think about all the horrible things that could have happened, she decided. *I'm only going to think of Aria standing there safe and calm in her corral, reaching her nose out to get her grain like she always does. She'll be happy to see me and she won't be mad at all. She'll forgive me for missing a day. She's the nicest horse I've ever known.*

The mountain lion had little luck with his hunt after leaving the Bright Creature the night before. The only living thing he saw besides the gray mare was a small jackrabbit he surprised at dawn. As the sun rose, he reluctantly took the rabbit back with him to hide in his hole in the rocks. He dreamed all day in his cool cavern, hidden away from hunters and from the desert heat.

The cat remembered a time when he hunted in the daylight too, but that was when he only killed for food. Shortly after he began doing it for sport, the humans began to find many bodies of dead cattle and horses, and started tracking him. That was when the big cat started to hide during the day and to kill at night.

When dusk returned and the sky over the desert turned red, he felt his blood rise within him. It was almost time to kill again. This time he would not be denied. He would find more than a measly rabbit.

The cat crept from his lair and, again, leapt to the top of the ridge. He raised his nose and sniffed for prey. Almost immediately he smelled deer. With a low growl, the lion dropped to the ground and crept toward his next victim.

I feel fear breaking over me in waves. No. Not fear. Terror! It is not a horse, but another creature. Aria feels it too, though not as powerfully. She stamps her hoof and sniffs the air, alert and watchful.

I will climb to the top of the canyon to see if I can find the terrorized creature. I must help it if I can.

The desert grew darker as Sophie walked. A few red streaks still illuminated the sky behind her, but they were fading fast. The cherry-colored light spilled over the sagebrush, casting long dark shadows behind each desert plant. Sophie did her best to ignore the pain in her body and arm. She remembered seeing a TV show where someone had said that when he was hurt he forced himself to believe it wasn't pain he felt, but merely sensation. *It's just a feeling,* concentrated Sophie. *It only hurts if I think of it as hurting, so it doesn't hurt. It doesn't hurt. It's only a sensation. Just like being touched. Or having Kalene brush my hair.*

When the moon rose over the mountains in front of her, Sophie was momentarily distracted. At first there was just a bright sliver above the tallest peak, then, slowly, slowly, it rose into the sky, large and luring. Its ivory glow touched the desert in front of her, turning the sagebrush from black to silver. The sight was almost enough to take her mind off of her aching arm. Almost, but not quite. *It's only a feeling. It doesn't hurt,* Sophie kept telling herself.

After walking for almost an hour, Sophie flopped the hay net on the ground and set the heavy bucket down beside it. She was getting so tired, and now even her good arm was aching. She stretched her left arm high above her head and then swung it in circles at her side, hoping to increase the circulation. Then she lowered herself to the ground and lay back on the soft hay.

40

She was only about a quarter of a mile away from the canyon now. The desert was breaking up into dry hills and arroyos and the rest of the way would be slower going. Aria's canyon was farther back in the hills, well hidden in the maze of precipices, arroyos, and canyons that made up the wild foothills. Behind them, arid mountains spiked to the sky.

I'll just lie here for a minute and rest, thought Sophie and shut her eyes. She cradled her broken arm carefully across her body and sighed. Life was getting way too complicated. She loved living with Kalene and Joel. She loved Aria and Rolly and the other horses. School was even okay and Max was great. Sophie was finally in a home where she felt appreciated, even loved, and sometimes she almost convinced herself she was a normal girl with a normal family.

When Sophie first realized Aria was in foal she knew she couldn't bear to lose Kalene and Joel. She couldn't bear to leave the ranch. That meant she couldn't tell them about what had happened, even though it was only a mistake. She couldn't take the chance that they might send her away. And her plan was almost complete. The foal would be born soon and would be old enough to wean in three or four months. She could keep it in the corral and feed it for a while after Aria was gone to make sure it was okay. That wasn't the hard part. The thing that would be tricky would be getting Aria back home without Kalene and Joel suspecting her.

There has to be a story Kalene and Joel will believe, thought Sophie. *There just has to be. And it's got to be good enough to fool them into thinking I had nothing to do with Aria's disappearance at all.*

The deer is dead, poor thing. At least her death was quick. Her terror did not last long. And the hunter ate, so he will not hunt again for a time. Though it is puzzling that he did not eat much. I wonder why? Did I frighten him away? No. He had moved on before I arrived.

And suddenly, I feel more anxiety in the air. It is the wild stallion, Sky. He has heard something near his herd and wonders if something threatens them. Could the hunter be stalking again? But that makes no sense. Why would he hunt again when he has just fed? Why would he wish to harm Sky and his herd? Unless he is more than just a hunter. Maybe he is a killer. Could he have been the dark creature near Aria last night? The one that is so twisted and malformed in spirit? So full of hate?

The herd is nervous. I can feel their unrest reaching out to me, calling me. They have sensed danger nearby, but Sky has not told them to run. Will he approach the killer to investigate, not knowing what it is until it's too late? I must hurry. I must warn them.

Sophie sighed. The hay net felt so soft and she was so tired. *I could fall asleep right here,* she thought. Then she opened her eyes. "I don't ever learn, do I?" she said aloud, her voice angry. "I'm such a loser! Last time I fell asleep in the desert, something awful happened and here I am doing it again!"

She climbed to her feet and bent to pick up the grain bucket, but then she froze. Was that a horse whinnying? Yes. The sound floated toward her again. *But I'm too far away from Aria's canyon to hear her,* Sophie thought. *Unless she escaped.* With a pounding heart, Sophie scanned the moonlit desert.

As soon as she spotted the wild horses, Sophie dropped to the ground. She knew the moment they saw her they would gallop away across the desert, dodging sagebrush and tumbleweed.

They haven't seen me yet, she realized when she didn't hear thundering hoofbeats. *That's strange, usually they're so watchful of danger. They're quite close. How could they miss me? They didn't even hear me when I spoke out loud.*

Slowly Sophie rose up far enough to see the wild horses again. She peered through the moonlit air, trying to count the mustangs, trying to pick out the one she remembered the most. The blue roan stallion. Big and rough and shaggy. She had only seen him once before, on the day he had stolen Aria away from her, but she knew she would never forget him.

44

The wild horses milled around, one large dark mass with many heads and tails. Nervous whinnies reached Sophie as the mares commanded their foals to stay near. *They're not looking in my direction,* Sophie realized. *They're looking toward the hills. And they're scared.*

A dark shape broke from the herd. It was the stallion! Sophie gasped as his powerful silhouette trotted toward the canyon cutting into the foothill, his long windswept mane and tail floating on the air behind him. Sophie knew it was the stallion's job to protect the herd. She guessed he was probably checking out a foreign smell or a strange noise to see if what he had sensed was dangerous.

The stallion drew closer to the shadows at the mouth of the canyon. He slowed and lowered his nose to the ground. Then he raised his proud head and snorted loudly. The sound echoed between the rocky walls.

Sophie held her breath. The stallion stood as still as a statue, his head high. Sophie imagined the breath rushing in and out of his nostrils as he read the signs, trying to understand what was wrong. His eyes would be sharp, looking into every shadow, every crevice in the rocks.

I don't see why they don't just turn and run, thought Sophie, but part of her was happy they didn't. *They're so beautiful and wild and free! They can't really be in danger. Nothing can hurt wild horses. They're way too fast.*

There he is. A mountain lion perched on the canyon lip. I will send tendrils of my energy toward him. I will try to frighten him away.

There, he sees me. Good! He is frightened of me. How quickly he fades into shadow. How completely he becomes hidden, as if he is made of darkness.

He is to be greatly feared. The bloodlust in him is overwhelming and pungent. It has consumed his soul. I know now he is the creature I sensed at Aria's enclosure. The feeling he leaves behind tells me so.

Oh Sky. My beautiful Sky. How glad I am that I was here! I am so relieved the mountain lion is afraid of me. But he may not be for much longer. You must avoid him, my lovely one. You must keep your herd safe.

My Sky. How glorious you are. Truly magnificent. The Great One smiled on the earth the day you were born! Allow me, please, to greet your family.

Sophie watched, mesmerized, as the stallion lowered his head and stepped into the shadow near the canyon wall. His soft neigh barely reached her as he greeted someone or something in the shadows. His walk was relaxed and his ears were forward as he disappeared into the darkness. He didn't even glance back at the mares.

What is he doing? thought Sophie. *Is he welcoming another wild horse? A mustang wouldn't approach any other kind of animal with a whinny, would it?* She watched the canyon entrance for a few minutes, unsure of what to do. She knew she should be making her way toward Aria. The mare would be waiting for her. But Sophie's curiosity was too strong. She had to see what would make the wild stallion walk into the canyon, especially when he'd been so nervous just moments before.

Abruptly the mares stopped circling. As one, they stepped toward the canyon, their heads down and their bodies at ease. Two of the foals rushed forward, jumping and playing. There were no whinnies from their dams warning them to stay back. At the entrance to the canyon, the mares formed a circle, some of them in shadow and some standing in the moonlight. Their heads pointed toward the center of their circle and their hindquarters faced outwards. Sophie saw movement in the shadows and thought it was the stallion joining the mares, but she wasn't sure. The shadows at the

canyon's entrance were too dark and the horses seemed to blend into a single form.

But still Sophie could tell the horses' actions weren't right. None of the books she'd read about mustangs mentioned that wild horses made formations like this. She knew they sometimes bunched together to protect themselves from danger when they couldn't run, but the herd wasn't milling about or jostling each other. They weren't panicky or frightened, with heads high, watching for danger. This was a perfect circle from what Sophie could see, with the horses standing quietly side by side. And the center of the circle was empty. Or was it?

Suddenly, Sophie's heart was beating like crazy. She dropped to the ground, breathless. There was something in the middle of the circle – something that shouldn't have been there!

Sophie inched up from the ground just enough to see the formation the horses had created. Her eyes tried to cut through the shadow but she just couldn't see clearly.

It was my imagination, she thought. *I couldn't have seen a person standing in the center of the ring of horses.*

No way. Mustangs would never let a human that close to them. Never.

After a few minutes, the herd began to break up. First the foals left the group and started to frolic, then the lead mare walked into the desert. The rest of the mares and foals followed loosely behind her. The stallion was the last to leave the canyon. When he finally trotted after the others, Sophie breathed a sigh of relief. The mustangs were acting normal again.

It was my imagination, Sophie told herself. *It was just a trick of the shadows. Or maybe it was a rock. But why would they be standing in a perfect circle around a rock? Or even stranger, nothing at all?* Sophie shivered and shoved the question to the back of her mind. *It was nothing,* she thought again. *I was just too far away to see clearly. And maybe the wild horse experts don't know everything there is to know about mustangs. After all, they can't get very close to them.*

Sophie waited to stand until the herd disappeared into the night and the sound of their hooves had faded. Her legs were stiff from crouching on the desert for so long. She shook them out, and then reached down for the hay net and oat bucket. Sophie was glad she didn't have too much farther to walk. After a short time her unbroken arm began aching again, tired from packing the hay and oats so far already.

Sophie searched the hills for the entrance to the large canyon that branched off into the narrow canyon where Aria was hidden. When she spotted the familiar rock formation marking the entrance and hurried toward it.

Carefully she walked into the shadows at the entrance to the canyon. The ground was broken and rough. The moonlight, so bright out on the open desert, couldn't reach the rocky floor and so the canyon was awash in darkness. Sophie stopped to wait for her eyes to adjust. Then she picked her way along the boulder-strewn ground. As she made her way inside, the walls became steeper. When the hilly edge of the canyon had turned to rock cliff, Sophie edged to one side and reached out. The rock wall was smooth beneath her fingers. Water from countless flash floods had blasted through this canyon over the centuries, wearing it into flowing patterns of stone.

She could tell how far she had traveled inside the canyon by looking up at the cliffs above her. She recognized many of the rock formations where the cliff's edge was dark against the moonlit sky. Finally she recognized the gap that marked the entrance to Aria's small canyon. She turned into it, put the oat bucket down and carried the hay net to the top of the steep rocky section. She threw it down beside the first willow bushes and turned back for the bucket.

Because the canyon was wider and elevated where the willows grew, the moonlight was able to touch them with its silver fingers. The trail to Aria's corral wound its way through the bushes like a glowing ribbon in front of Sophie, and the tinkling sound of water greeted her from the tangled depths of vegetation.

I'm almost there, Sophie thought with relief when she heard the spring. *I'm so tired!*

The first time she'd walked into the narrow canyon stretching off the larger, barren one, Sophie knew she had found the perfect place to build Aria's corral. The entrance

51

to the smaller canyon was narrow with high bluffs on either side. This would make anyone who saw it think the canyon was smaller than it was. But after the narrow opening, the rocky floor rose and the canyon widened. Willow bushes grew wall to wall as thick as hair on a dog's back and almost impenetrable.

But what made it perfect for Aria was the hidden spring. Artesian water bubbled out of the ground like magic, springing out near the narrow crevice at the back of Aria's enclosure and pooling among the rocks. From the pool, it traveled less than two hundred yards, through Aria's enclosure and into the willow thicket, before it sank back into the dry ground.

It had taken Sophie a long time to clear out enough bushes to make a trail wide enough for Aria to walk, and then to clear out a corral for her. She wove most of the willow bushes she removed into the living willow at the edge of the enclosure to make a natural fence.

The rest of the displaced willow was packed into the narrow crevice running through the rock wall at the back of Aria's enclosure. The crevice was a narrow slit in the rocks that led to a steep, dangerous trail, covered with loose stones, that dropped down to the main canyon again. Sophie knew when she sealed the crevice that she was blocking off the trail the local deer used to access the spring water, but she had no choice. She needed to keep Aria from using the crevice to escape back to the ranch. It would be terrible if Aria was discovered in foal, but even worse, if she slipped on the narrow rocky trail and fell to the main canyon below.

Sophie felt badly about the deer at first, and hoped they'd be able to find water elsewhere. She was pleasantly surprised to find that the willow fence didn't even slow them down. Finding the path through the crevice blocked, they made their way down the trail that Sophie cleared through the willows. They leapt over the willow gate and, despite Aria's presence, proceeded to drink at the pool. Sophie found their tracks in the dust on the trail and had even surprised them there a time or two.

Now she moved stiffly along the trail, trying to ignore her aching arms. Then the willow gate was in front of her. Sighing gratefully, she plopped her load down.

"Aria," she called, bending to crawl through the hole in the tightly woven willow gate. "Aria, I'm here."

Silence.

Sophie crawled through the opening and climbed to her feet. "Aria?" she said. The corral spread out before her. Aria's gray bulk stood at the far end. Her head was in shadows.

"Aria?" whispered Sophie, suddenly feeling the hair on the back of her neck raise up. *Why isn't she neighing to me? Isn't she happy to see me?*

"Aria, I have your oats," said Sophie and knelt to pull the bucket through the hole. Then she reached back for the hay net. Slowly she carried them both toward Aria.

The gray mare still stood with her hindquarters facing Sophie. Sophie stopped. Something wasn't right. Aria never acted this way. She was always happy to see Sophie. Could she be mad that Sophie took so long to come feed her?

Then Sophie noticed that the mare was eating something. Fresh hay lay on the ground in front of her.

"What?" whispered Sophie. "How did you get hay?"

Sophie lowered the bucket to the ground and tried not to scream. Someone was standing behind her. She wasn't sure how she knew – she could just feel it.

Slowly she turned around. A girl stood beside the willow gate. Her face seemed luminous and, even in the pale moon-

53

light, Sophie could see that her eyes were a strange amber color. Her hair was long and drifted in a breeze that Sophie couldn't feel. *Her hair is glowing gold, not silver like the moonlight should make it look,* Sophie realized. A wave of fear washed over her. She opened her mouth to speak but the old terror suddenly grabbed her tongue and she couldn't say anything.

Instead it was the girl who spoke, her voice as soft and gentle as a summer wind. "Aria has missed you," she said. "You cannot leave her in this hidden place. You must take her home."

The girl is so frightened. I wish I could have approached her in the daylight. Everything is so much scarier in the dark, especially for humans. But I cannot wait until tomorrow. I must tell her of the danger that is here. The danger that may, once again, stalk Aria and her foal, little Melody. I can tell this girl is the one who is meant to save Aria and Melody. Their lives are in her hands alone.

Is this girl strong enough to do what needs to be done? Can she return them to their owners? To do so, she must face her worst fear. Is she brave enough? Strong enough?

I pray that she will be so, or... or Aria and Melody will be the next victims of a ruthless killer.

Sophie drew in a sharp breath and stepped backward. She felt Aria's warm side behind her and pressed back against the mare as she watched the strange girl.

The girl stepped toward her. "Do not be frightened," she said. "I am not here to hurt you. Only to help."

All Sophie could do was shake her head. She knew this girl wouldn't help. She had already said that Sophie had to take Aria home. This girl was going to ruin her life; this girl whose life was surely perfect, with her long golden hair, perfect face, and her startling tawny eyes. This was the girl who would tell Kalene and Joel about Aria.

They'll hate me when they find out, thought Sophie. *They won't even want to look at me.* In her mind, Sophie watched the love that she had seen in Kalene's eyes replaced by the pain caused by her foster daughter's betrayal. She imagined hearing Joel's voice saying, "How can we ever trust you again, Sophie?" And then the shuffle from one foster home to another would start. Again.

I wish I were dead, thought Sophie. *I wish God would just make an earthquake swallow me up, right here. Right now. Then I would never have to see them turn away.*

Slowly she sank to her knees beside Aria and covered her face with her left hand, but she was too wretched to cry. She felt Aria nuzzle her shoulder.

"I am sorry to have frightened you," said a voice above

her, but Sophie couldn't look up. She knew what she would see in the girl's eyes. Accusations.

Exactly like the accusations in Sophie's mother's eyes on the day she walked out the door and never came back. Though Sophie had only been six years old then, her mother had blamed her for ruining her life. That was when Sophie had first wondered if she was poison to those who loved her. During the days that followed, alone in the apartment she had once shared with her mother, she kept wondering, too afraid to leave and hungry, hungry, hungry. Sophie started to believe what her mom had said. It *was* all her fault. She had destroyed her mother's life simply by being born. By existing.

By the time the neighbors grew suspicious and called the authorities, Sophie had been alone for almost a week. She was scrawny, dirty, and terrified when she was found. Immediately, the social workers placed her in a foster home. The damage to her body was quickly corrected with medical attention and good food, but her mind was unreachable. She was too afraid to even speak. A succession of foster parents were nice to her, hoping to be the ones that helped her, but in the end they always gave up. Sophie became like a shadow in their homes, quiet and watchful. Afraid.

And her fear always came true; they always sent her on to another home. After six years of bouncing from one place to another, Sophie was ready to give up on herself.

But then Kalene and Joel had come into her life, and welcomed her into their home with open arms. When Sophie was silent, they didn't try to force her to speak. They just accepted her the way she was. And Sophie started to accept herself.

The day finally came, months later, when Sophie realized she could trust them. It was the day they told her she could ride Aria. Aria was the obvious choice for a riding horse, being the only mare not in foal on the ranch, but Sophie was still surprised. Aria was their most valuable mare, the one they could least afford to lose. Yet they trusted Sophie with the beautiful gray mare anyway.

It was a real blow to them when the mare disappeared, without a trace. *And now they are going to find out that I'm the thief,* thought Sophie. *They're going to learn the truth about me. The truth my mom knew when she walked out on me. The truth that all those other foster parents learned about me. I'm poison. I destroy people's lives.*

Overwhelmed by despair, Sophie sunk to the ground and sobs wracked her body. She felt Aria's muzzle on her back again and then the warm hand of the girl.

They don't know what I'm really like, thought Sophie, her mind ravaged with guilt. *If they did, they wouldn't be nice to me. Aria still likes me because she's a horse and horses don't understand things like betrayal. She doesn't realize that she's here, stuck in this canyon away from all her friends and her safe barn, because of me. And the girl, she just doesn't know what I'm like yet. She doesn't know what a horrible person I am.*

The girl's hand lay between Sophie's shoulder blades, warm and comforting. When Sophie's sobs slowed and her breath became quieter and shallower, she finally pulled her hand away.

After a few minutes, Sophie rubbed her eyes and wiped her tears on her jeans, then she inhaled deeply and sat up straight. She looked up into Aria's moon-washed face glowing above her. The mare whinnied and nuzzled her again. "I'm so sorry girl," whispered Sophie. "I'm so sorry all this happened. You didn't deserve this, did you?"

"She is very worried about you," said the girl.

Sophie turned. The girl was sitting on the ground, almost

behind her. When Sophie met the strange girl's gaze, the girl smiled. Quickly Sophie turned away. "Are you going to tell them about Aria?" she asked in a choked voice.

"Tell who about Aria?" asked the girl, her voice gently inquisitive.

Sophie sighed. *There's no point in not letting her know,* she thought. *All she has to do is go to the police to ask who is missing an Arabian mare.*

"Her owners," Sophie finally said. "My foster parents, Kalene and Joel James." When the girl did not immediately answer her, Sophie turned. The girl was staring at the edge of the canyon, watching the black ridge top.

Hope surged through Sophie. *Maybe she won't tell. Maybe she'll just go away and leave Aria and me alone. I mean, it's not like I'm not going to return Aria anyway. I've just got to wait until her foal is weaned, that's all.*

Finally the girl turned back to Sophie. "You must return Aria now," she stated simply.

Sophie's fresh hope was crushed. "But…" she started to say.

The girl held up a slim hand. "Wait. Listen," she said. "You must return Aria in the morning because she is in danger here. A mountain lion has moved into these hills." The girl's graceful hand waved toward the bluff. "He is not a normal mountain lion, but a killer who feeds off the fear of his victims. He knows Aria is here. I have frightened him away once already, but I do not know how much longer I can keep him at bay."

"Did he try to attack her? Is she okay?" asked Sophie and scrambled to her feet. "He didn't hurt her, did he?" Sophie's hand explored Aria's body. She was relieved to feel nothing but silky softness beneath her hands. No cuts. No scratches.

"He did not hurt her," said the strange girl. "He is afraid

of me. For now. But I have no doubt he will be back. You must take Aria home. Tomorrow. As soon as the sun shines on the hills. You are in danger too, as you walk to and from Aria's enclosure."

"But how can I take her home?" asked Sophie turning back to the girl. "I can't let Kalene and Joel know that I stole her. They'll send me away."

The girl's golden eyes searched Sophie's face. Then she patted the ground beside her. "There is great kindness in you," she said. "And great fear. Come. Sit. Tell me why you have stolen Aria away. I will listen."

Sophie sank to the ground beside the girl. For a few seconds, she stared at her own hands folded in her lap. The old fear of speaking crept up behind her and wrapped its silent hands across her mouth, around her throat. Sophie looked up into the girl's eyes imploringly, begging not to have to tell her about Aria. "Who are you?" Sophie suddenly blurted out. It was easier to ask questions than tell the girl her story. "Where do you live? I've never seen you here before." Then, before the girl could reply, she added in a softer voice, "I'm Sophie, by the way."

"Hi Sophie. My name is Angelica," said the girl. "And I do not live here. I come from far away."

A deeper curiosity grew inside Sophie as she listened to Angelica. Though Angelica had replied to Sophie's questions, her answers hadn't really told Sophie anything. "From where?" she tried again.

"From a different place," said Angelica. "It is hard to explain."

"A different country?" asked Sophie.

"Yes, you could say that," was Angelica's answer.

"How did you find Aria?" Sophie asked in frustration, trying to understand. "Why did you come here?"

"I came to help her," Angelica said in answer to Sophie's second question.

"What do you mean?"

"I will tell you, but first you must tell me your story. That is the most important thing now. Who I am or where I come from does not matter. We must make a plan to save Aria."

Sophie's eyes searched Angelica's face. Even though Angelica hadn't really answered any of her questions, there was something about the older girl that she trusted. There was a quietness about her. A peace.

And I have nothing to lose, she reminded herself. *Maybe I'll even be able to talk her out of making me return Aria. She might know some other way to keep Aria safe from the mountain lion.*

"Okay," agreed Sophie, but then her voice faltered.

"Well?" asked Angelica, prompting her. Sophie drew a deep breath. Aria moved from the oat bucket and sniffed at the hay. Without a word, Sophie stood and picked up the hay net from where she had dropped it. She tied it in its usual place, glad for the small interruption, and then reluctantly turned back to where Angelica waited. Taking her courage in hand, she lowered herself to the ground again and began to speak.

It didn't take long to tell the entire story. When she was done, Sophie looked up at the sky. The moon hung over them like a huge, glowing coin. Sophie closed her eyes and, with her head still tipped back, took a deep breath of the silver air. Then she asked the question that was eating at her. "Are you going to tell Joel and Kalene about Aria? Are you going to tell them what I've done?"

Angelica was silent for a long moment as she too, watched the moon hang in the night sky. Then she turned to Sophie.

"No," she said. "You are."

62

The mountain lion glared at the creatures below from his safe perch on the top of the canyon wall. He wasn't sure why he'd returned, especially after he'd been so frightened the night before. All he knew was that the fear inside him had turned to rage. An unreasonable, hate-filled, black anger that ate at him from the inside and wouldn't let go.

He could tell they hadn't noticed him yet. Even the horse hadn't sensed him. He'd been very careful to stay downwind, careful to contain his energy. The lion growled quietly as he watched the Bright Creature, the human, and the horse.

The horse would be no problem to kill. He'd done it before. Even if it were big and fast, once he was on its back, it wouldn't have a chance to escape. It would be almost too easy.

But the human? He had never killed a human. He always wondered how strong they were. This one didn't look as strong as the hunters. It was much smaller for one thing and its arm seemed to be trapped inside a fat white bone. But, most importantly, it didn't have a fire stick. The big cat had seen a human with a fire stick kill a coyote once. The human had aimed the fire stick at the coyote, there had been a loud noise and the coyote had fallen, dead. The lion's eyes analyzed the small human. Yes, he was sure he could take it down as long as

63

it didn't have a fire stick. It might even be the easiest to kill.

The Bright Creature was the one he didn't know about. He didn't even know what it was, let alone how to best attack it. The lion growled again as he stared at the creature. It really didn't look very strong. It too, was smaller than the hunters, smaller than the horses and cattle he had slaughtered. Could it be stronger than them? Stronger than him? Eagerly the cat leaned forward. No, he didn't think so. But it might put up a good fight. So many of his victims died too easily, long before his blood-thirst was satisfied.

The lion's tongue darted from between his glistening teeth to taste the blood of the deer, metallic and strong, on his jaw. He could hear his heart pounding in anticipation of the hunt. With a low, resonating rumble in his chest, he lowered himself flat to the ground and crept forward.

"What do you mean?" asked Sophie, aghast, her hopes dashed. "I can't tell them. I'm *not* going to tell them! Didn't you hear me? If they know, they'll send me away." Sophie felt tears threaten to spring from her eyes again, but she didn't care.

Angelica didn't respond. Instead she looked up at the bluff. Her eyes ran along the top of the canyon wall.

A trickle of fear slid down Sophie's spine and she searched the darkness with Angelica. "What is it?" she whispered. "What's wrong?"

"He is here. Somewhere. I cannot tell where," Angelica whispered in return. In one fluid movement she was on her feet, her golden hair rippling in the soft light. When Sophie opened her mouth to speak, Angelica raised her hand to silence her again. The older girl listened for a moment, staring off into the darkness. Then a low whistle came from her lips. Immediately Aria left her hay and trotted toward them.

"Come," whispered Angelica and motioned to Sophie to move to the center of the clearing with them. "Quickly."

Sophie didn't hesitate. She jumped to her feet and hurried to stand beside Aria.

"Stand by her head and keep her from running away, no matter what. She must not panic and run toward the willows or the rocks. She must stay in the open," commanded Angelica.

"What is it?" asked Sophie, although she had a good idea.

Angelica confirmed her suspicion. "It is the mountain lion. He is stalking us. I think he intends to attack."

"How do you…" Sophie began to ask, but Angelica interrupted her with the answer to her question.

"I can feel his evil drawing nearer. I can feel his desire to kill like a black mist in the air." With that she left Aria's side and walked cautiously toward the shadows at the edge of the enclosure. "He is very close," she added, without turning back to Sophie. "I will stay between you and him, but first I must discover from which direction he comes."

Sophie stood at Aria's head and waited. Suddenly, she spun around and looked into the black night behind her. *What if the mountain lion attacks from behind when Angelica is in front of us?* she thought. She turned back toward Angelica with worried eyes. *Or what if it springs out of the darkness to attack Angelica?* Sophie watched the older girl walk in a circle around the enclosure, her golden eyes probing the shadows.

Angelica made a full turn around the two in the center before she looked back at Sophie. "He is very near, but I cannot tell from which direction he comes. And I do not dare lead Aria from the enclosure. The trail to the open desert is too narrow and we would be too vulnerable."

Sophie's fear mounted. It was hard to breathe. "What do we do?" The question rushed out, even though her tongue felt like rubber.

"Stay in the middle of the enclosure, away from the canyon walls and the underbrush. He may jump from above or rush from below. Either attack could be deadly," said Angelica. "I will continue to circle. He was afraid of me before. Maybe he still is, a little."

"No," protested Sophie. "You stand with us, beside Aria. What if the mountain lion waits until you are on the opposite side and then attacks us? We should stick together. It'll be more afraid of us if we're in a group."

Angelica paused, her face undecided for a moment. Finally she spoke. "I will stand with you until I can tell from which direction he comes."

"Okay," said Sophie, relieved. She felt so much better with the older girl near, even though Angelica was probably as helpless as she was against a crazed mountain lion.

Angelica moved to stand to one side of Aria while Sophie stood on the other. They listened in the silence for a sound, any sound, that might give an idea of where the cat might be. Sophie tried to see into the shadows at the edge of the enclosure. She didn't notice any signs of life, but after a moment her eyes made out the shape of a large stick lying a few feet away from the edge of a clump of thick willow. *I need something to fight back with,* thought Sophie. *It'll only take a second to grab the stick and get back to Aria. Then I can protect her better.*

With a quiet step, Sophie moved toward the stick. She'd just reached it when she heard Angelica's urgent whisper behind her. "What are you doing, Sophie? The lion could be anywhere."

Sophie looked back. "I need something to fight with and this stick is big enough. Then I can hit the mountain lion if it jumps at Aria," she explained, turning away from Angelica to pick up the club.

Angelica yelled "No!" at the very moment Sophie saw something move. Like dark liquid, the large cat flowed toward her, low to the ground. A terrifying rumble erupted from its chest. Sophie saw its fangs gleaming in the moonlight. Her heart hammered as her fingers groped for the wood.

The beast stopped a few feet away from Sophie and

glared at her, unblinking. Slowly Sophie straightened and swung the stick into position as if she was ready to play baseball. She began to walk slowly backward. A strange buzzing filled her ears.

Then everything seemed to happen at once. The lion leapt toward Sophie, just as an explosion of light burst from behind her, sweeping around and through her body to reach the big cat. The explosion pushed Sophie toward the mountain lion, but it seemed to affect the creature even more. In mid-spring he was blown back. As Sophie tumbled to the ground, she felt the brightness coursing through her like a lightening bolt. Her whole body tingled. But it wasn't a bad feeling. In fact it was wonderful. Sophie had never felt so alive, so vibrant. Her heart throbbed. Her breath came in gasps and, even lying on the ground, she felt dizzy and light-headed. And fantastic. Absolutely fantastic.

Slowly the tingling feeling faded. With surprising ease, Sophie pushed herself into a sitting position and searched the underbrush. The cat was gone.

What on earth was that? she wondered as she climbed to her feet. *What happened?* She turned to the center of the enclosure to find Aria standing calmly, her head lowered.

Angelica lay at the mare's hooves, crumpled into a heap. Her arms lay limply on the ground and her hair spilled across the dry desert ground like a silken mantle, white in the moonlight and drained of all its vibrant color.

Gone. Energy gone.

But I had to save her. I would do it again. If I could.

Aria is here. I feel her presence like a living flame. Will she save me? Only she can. I am at her mercy.

My light is going out. . .

Sophie ran to Angelica's side, knelt beside her and picked up her pale, limp hand. "Angelica!" she said loudly. With an effort, she calmed her voice. She leaned over the fallen girl. "Angelica, are you okay? Can I help? Tell me what's wrong so I can help! Please, Angelica. You've got to be okay. What happened?"

When Aria touched Sophie with her muzzle the first time, Sophie hardly noticed. The next time, Aria gently but firmly put her muzzle against Sophie's shoulder and pushed her back. Sophie fell backward, catching herself with her left arm. She looked at Aria with amazement. Aria had never done anything aggressive in all the months Sophie had known her.

With wide eyes, Sophie watched the gray mare lower her head and blow gently through her nostrils onto Angelica's stricken face. Angelica didn't move. It was as if she was dead, but Sophie couldn't see a mark on her. The mountain lion hadn't come near her. Sophie looked back at the willows where she had last seen the big cat. It was still gone. She turned back just in time to notice something fall onto Angelica's marble cheek. A tiny crystal drop. Then another. Around each miniscule drop, Angelica's skin lost its ivory paleness, the new color spreading outward like ripples on a pond.

Sophie gasped. The water drops were coming from Aria.

The mare was crying. Two wet tracks of tears were running down her face and the tears were dripping onto Angelica. And they were curing her from whatever made her fall. Sophie watched life return to Angelica's face and spread to her hair, turning it from silver-white back to gold.

Aria loves her, thought Sophie. *That's what's curing Angelica. Aria's love. But Aria hardly knows her. How could she love her so fast?*

Suddenly, the image of the wild horses standing in their perfect circle leapt into Sophie's mind and she understood. The mountain lion had been stalking them and Angelica had scared it away. Then the herd had come forward to greet her. They had no fear of her. They loved her, just as Aria did. Maybe all horses loved Angelica.

Angelica's eyes opened and Sophie moved farther away. Angelica smiled weakly and struggled to a sitting position.

"Who are you? *What* are you?" asked Sophie quietly. Aria nickered to Angelica and snuffled in her hair. "Are you an alien? Or magic? Or an angel? What?"

"I am Angelica. Only Angelica," said the girl, reaching up to stroke Aria's nose. "I do not know how else to say it. I am simply myself. It is only what I do that is unusual."

"What do you do then?" asked Sophie.

"I save horses. I am brought, no – pulled, to where I am needed by the horses themselves. That is my calling, my job. When you did not come to Aria last night, she was frightened that something had happened to you. Which I see it did." Angelica reached out and brushed her fingers along Sophie's cast, then pulled her hand away. "She was also frightened by the mountain lion. And she was frightened for Melody, afraid of what might happen if she came before her time and no one was here."

"Melody? Who is Melody?" asked Sophie in confusion.

72

"Aria's foal. The one she carries," explained Angelica. "The filly foal by Sky, the wild stallion."

"Sky? The mustang stallion has a name? And Melody? She has a name already? Did you name her?" asked Sophie, sounding flustered.

"The wild herd sire is named Sky. And who chose Melody's name is not important," said Angelica apologetically. "I am sorry to confuse you but it is so hard to explain these things. And what really matters is that Aria was frightened and she pulled me to her. And now my job is to save her and her foal."

"And me?" asked Sophie, softly. "Is it your job to save me? Because you did, didn't you? That light. It was from you, wasn't it? It killed the mountain lion."

"No, I did not kill him," said Angelica and shook her head. "I would not kill him if I could. Even though he has let evil overcome him, it would be wrong to take his life from him."

"But the light was from you," said Sophie again. A statement, not a question.

"Yes," said Angelica. "I sent my light. All of it in a single burst. It threw the mountain lion back and he was afraid, so he ran. He did not have to run. It was his choice and we were lucky that was the choice he made."

"And then after you sent your light, you didn't have any left," said Sophie, quietly. "Were you dying?" When there was no reply, she answered her own question in a whisper. "You were. You saved me, even though it could have killed you." Suddenly, Sophie couldn't speak. The magnitude of Angelica's gift flooded through her and she felt a lump in her throat. "Why would you do that?" she managed to say.

"Death is not the end you think it is, Sophie," said Angelica softly. "Only the physical part of me can be hurt

73

when my power is spent. There are many who would sacrifice to save you, Sophie. Aria would have if she could. And I believe your foster parents would as well. I think you underestimate your worth to them. You underestimate their love for you." She put her hand on Sophie's shoulders. "I know you do not want to tell your foster parents you have taken Aria because of your fear that they will send you away. But maybe they will not."

"How can you say that? How can you know?" asked Sophie in a choked voice.

"I do not know. I wish I did," said Angelica. "I wish I could tell you for certain that everything was going to be okay. But they sound like kind people. They seem to care for you very much."

"Can't you just *know,* like you know Aria's foal is a filly and that her name is Melody?" asked Sophie, her eyes hopeful.

"I know those things because I know Melody. I understand horses and, though Melody is not born yet, she is still here. I know the name she chooses for herself and why," explained Angelica. "But I do not understand people in the same way. Like you, I can only make the best judgement I can."

"Why did Melody choose that name?" asked Sophie. She wanted to think about something besides Joel and Kalene, about anything other than being sent away.

Angelica smiled. "Melody has heard sounds even from inside her dam. She has heard the wind playing in the willows and the brook bubbling from the ground and splashing out of the pool. She has heard the hawk's cry and the whisper of the deer as they come to the spring to drink. And your voice. She has heard your voice speaking kind words to Aria, words of encouragement and love. To her, these

74

sounds are like music and she wishes to be named for the songs she has heard."

"The songs of the desert," said Sophie, in a soft voice. "Like a quiet lullaby. A melody. She sounds like a beautiful foal."

"She is," said Angelica. "And she trusts you to take care of her. You and Aria."

Sophie sighed and scuffed the ground with her shoe. There was no way out of it. She had to keep Aria and Melody safe from the mountain lion, no matter what, and the only way to do that was to return them to the ranch.

I'll have to take the chance that Angelica might be right, realized Sophie. *It means I have to trust that Joel and Kalene love me enough to forgive me. And if they don't, well at least Aria and Melody will be safe. Melody should grow up as a tame horse anyway. Then she'll always have food, and no crazy mountain lions will be after her.* Sophie grimaced, thinking through the rest of her decision. *Even if Joel and Kalene sell her because she's only half Arabian, they'll find a good home for her. And if they send me away, I'll just go. It's not like they were going to adopt me or anything. I would've had to leave sometime, anyway; Child Services always takes me away in the end.*

With pained eyes, Sophie looked up into Angelica's beautiful face. For a moment the words stuck in her mouth, then she forced herself to say what she dreaded to say. "I'll tell them." She shuddered uncontrollably for a second, then she said it again, more to herself than to Angelica. "I'll tell Joel and Kalene what I've done."

The mountain lion was thrown back against the underbrush. As soon as he regained his feet, he ran from the Bright Creature as fast as he could. Finally, out of breath and miles away, he came to a stop. His limbs still trembled from the power that had assaulted him. The burst of light had swept through every cell in his body, shaking and invading the lion to the core, screaming through all of his killing fantasies, surrounding every murderous thought and flooding it with what the lion hated more than anything. Goodness. Love.

The lion retched. Within moments his stomach was empty. He looked back over his shoulder in the direction of the canyon. He would kill the Bright Creature. None of the others mattered now. None of the others had violated him like the Bright Creature had. He would kill it. Make no mistake.

But not now. Not tonight. The light it sent forth had sapped his strength and he needed rest. But as soon as his strength was restored, he would hunt again.

And there was only one he would hunt this time. Only one that he needed to slaughter. The Bright Creature. He would either have it or would die trying.

After the decision to return Aria was made, Sophie was surprised at how relieved she felt. She hadn't realized how much the guilt of hiding Aria from Kalene and Joel was weighing upon her until she finally decided to end her deception.

Sophie agreed to Angelica's suggestion to leave Aria in the canyon for the night. Aria seemed tired from all the excitement. A light sweat glistened on her shoulders and she seemed restless and worried. Sophie certainly didn't want to risk walking her back across the desert in the dark. Sophie knew Aria felt comfortable in the canyon. She'd spent many peaceful, but lonely, nights there and, even though Angelica had said the mountain lion was only frightened, Sophie was sure he wouldn't be back. The light that swept through her had changed her somehow, and she believed it must have affected the big cat too – maybe even more than it had her.

After Sophie gave Aria a goodbye hug, she and Angelica crawled through the hole in the woven willow gate and walked down the canyon toward the desert floor. When they reached the steep rock walls Angelica looked up at the cliffs above them. Sophie followed her eyes, but couldn't see anything except the cliff edge.

They walked in silence for a few minutes, then Angelica spoke. "One thing I must ask of you Sophie," she said in a serious voice. "I must ask you to please not tell anyone about me."

"Why not?" asked Sophie, though the thought hadn't

crossed her mind. How could she tell Kalene and Joel about the magical things she had seen tonight? They would think she was crazy. Sophie didn't even think Max would believe her.

"I am here to help the horses and sometimes, when too many people are involved, that becomes harder," replied Angelica. "We must save Aria and Melody together, without your foster parents' help."

"Don't worry, I won't tell anyone," Sophie promised gladly.

Within a few minutes, they reached the barren canyon. They followed it as it widened and the rock walls turned to hills. The desert stretched out before them, miles and miles of sagebrush glowing silver in the moonlight. Sophie looked up at the moon and noticed it was much higher in the sky.

"Oh no," she said. "I'll never make it home before Joel and Kalene get there. Poor Max is going to be in so much trouble."

"You are not walking home, Sophie," said Angelica. A low whistle came from her lips, then she spoke again. "Not when there is a mountain lion prowling about."

Then Sophie saw him. Sky. The wild stallion trotted toward them across the desert. Giddiness washed over her as he drew nearer. Angelica went to meet him, her hands outstretched. The two stopped when they met and the stallion dipped his powerful head, placing his muzzle into Angelica's hands. Then he stepped forward and pushed his face against her body. Angelica's hands stroked his neck and she leaned toward his ear. Sophie heard the wind rustling the sagebrush around her, but nothing more. Then Angelica stepped back and motioned for Sophie to come forward.

Cautiously Sophie walked toward the wild stallion. She had never been so close to a wild horse before and when he snorted at her approach, she stopped short. The first time she had seen Sky, the day he had stolen Aria away, she had been impressed with his power and energy. Up close, he was even more impressive. His mane was shaggy and tangled, and his forelock hung in a long clump down his roman nose. His eyes were watchful and wary; his neck was thick and set well into muscular shoulders. The rest of his body was muscular as well, but Sophie noticed he was quite thin. She could easily count his ribs, with the groove between each rib falling in shadow.

"He will not hurt you," said Angelica. "You can come closer."

When she reached Angelica's side, Sophie stopped again. Slowly, she reached out and touched the dark roan face. The stallion looked at Sophie with inquisitive, unafraid eyes and his expression made Sophie wonder if he was as curious about humans as she was about wild horses.

"Sky will take you home," said Angelica. "He can take you much faster than you can walk and I can stay with Aria in the canyon and keep her safe."

"He'll let me ride him?" breathed Sophie. Her fingers lingered on his face, trailing downward toward his nose. "He'll actually let me sit on him and ride him?" she repeated.

"Yes. He has agreed to do so," said Angelica.

"But he's a wild horse," said Sophie taking a step back, totally confused. "How can he agree to anything?"

Angelica smiled. "Humans are not the only creatures who can think or promise something or even give a gift. Sky is giving you a gift, a ride home, because he is grateful to you for caring for Aria all these months. He will not buck you off. He promises."

"This is like a dream," said Sophie. "But an awesome dream! Riding a wild horse? How many people can say they've done that? This is amazing!"

Beside her, Angelica laughed. "Come. You must hurry, remember?" she said. "I will give you a leg up."

Sky stood still as a statue as Angelica and Sophie moved to his side. Sophie was surprised he wasn't as tall as she had imagined him to be. *He has such a strong presence,* she realized, *that he seems bigger than he really is.*

Within a few seconds, she was sitting astride the horse. His back was broad, and, as soon as she was aboard, Sophie reached for his mane with her good hand. "He's amazing," she whispered, then gasped as the stallion began to walk. "Does he know where I live?" she called back to Angelica.

"You can guide him by using leg signals, just like any other horse," Angelica said behind her. "I will see you tomorrow morning, Sophie. And do not worry. I will keep Aria safe."

Sophie waved to Angelica. Then she turned forward and gently pressed her foot to Sky's side. He turned slightly to the right as he walked. "Who taught you how to do that, boy?" Sophie asked, not expecting a response. She always talked to the horses at the ranch and talking to Sky came just as naturally.

"You're amazing," continued Sophie, stroking his shoulder. Sky moved at a quick pace, sweeping around sagebrush and stepping over holes smoothly and effortlessly. Though Sophie had ridden Aria many times in the desert, it hadn't been like this. Aria had always walked carefully, but she had never moved like Sky. She didn't move as if she belonged there, as if the desert was an extension of who she was. Sky was like a ballet dancer on the stage, graceful and flowing, his stride long and smooth and elastic.

Sophie cautiously squeezed her heels against his side. Instantly, the mustang broke into an extended trot, his head up and ears forward. Sophie clung to his mane with her

good hand and bounced. Then she squeezed his side with her knees once more and he broke into a rocking horse canter.

Sophie couldn't believe how free she felt as they raced across the desert. Sky was beyond amazing! The entire night was like a dream, except no dream ever ended this wonderfully. Sophie wished they would never reach Joel and Kalene's house. They could gallop across the desert forever. When she saw the lights in the distance, Sky seemed to recognize her mood and slowed to a walk. They approached the pasture behind the house and when they reached the fence, Sky stopped. He raised his head and sniffed the air.

"Can you smell the other horses, boy?" asked Sophie and patted his neck. She hated the thought of slipping from his strong back. *But Joel and Kalene are going to be home soon,* she reminded herself. *I can't leave Max to face them alone. I've got to get into the house before they come.*

Slowly, she slid from Sky's back. She leaned on his side for a moment and inhaled his horsey scent, then moved forward to his head. "Thanks, Sky," she said, her words simple and heartfelt. "I'll remember you forever." She kissed him on the forehead. Sky only snorted, then, when Sophie stepped back, he spun away and leapt into a gallop. Sophie watched him with a lump in her throat as he raced away.

When Sky was gone Sophie turned away and climbed through the fence. She was halfway across the pasture when she realized her arm didn't hurt any more. Not a single ache, not even the tiniest pain. She tightened her muscles under her cast, but her arm felt as strong as it was before her accident. And the rest of her body felt normal, too. None of her scrapes and bruises hurt.

How strange, she thought. *I figured being hit by a car would take longer than a day to stop hurting.*

It is Aria's time.

Melody will be born tonight.

How blessed I am to be here. How privileged I am to be their protector. Oh my Great One, thank you. Thank you with all of my heart.

Sophie hurried into the house. Twixie met her at the door, her tail whipping back and forth, threatening to wallop anyone who came within range of its swing. She greeted Sophie with a long whine and spun in a circle, whacking her on the leg with her tail.

Max rushed in from the living room. "What took you so long?" she asked, her face a mask of worry. "I was ready to go looking for you!"

"Sorry," said Sophie. "I tried to hurry." She reached down and grabbed Twixie's tail with her hand. "Sit Twixie," she commanded. The overexcited dog whined again, then plopped her bottom onto the floor.

"Was Aria okay?" asked Max, relaxing a little.

"Yeah, she was fine," said Sophie. "And I'm starved. Come to the kitchen and I'll tell you the rest."

"Did something else happen?" asked Max behind Sophie. Twixie followed the two of them into the kitchen, her tail still swinging from side to side.

Sophie bit her lip. It was so hard to keep Angelica a secret. And Sky, too. She was dying to tell Max about riding Sky across the desert but she couldn't. She had promised not to tell anyone about Angelica, and she could hardly tell Max about Sky without including Angelica in the story. But there was something she could tell Max. "I decided I'm going to bring Aria home," she said. "Tomorrow."

"What?" asked Max, surprised. "Why?"

I can't tell Max about Aria being in danger either, because then I'd need to explain why I didn't bring her home tonight. "I'm afraid something will happen to the foal," Sophie said, as she reached for the peanut butter in the cupboard. "Now that my arm's broken, I won't be able to get out there as much, and I'm afraid Aria will foal when I'm not there. It's her first time, and that's when mares have the most difficulty. Aria and Melody's safety is the most important thing."

"Melody," said Max. "Who's Melody?"

"Umm, she's the foal," said Sophie, embarrassed.

"You named her already?" Max asked.

"Yeah," answered Sophie, her face pink. She wished she'd caught the mistake before it slipped out of her mouth. "I know it's silly," she added.

"No, it's not," said Max, removing two pieces of bread from the bread bag and handing them to Sophie. "A lot of people name their babies before they're born. Why not a foal? I just hope it's a filly. Melody is a goofy name for a colt."

Sophie smiled gratefully at her friend. "Can you spread the peanut butter on for me too? I can't do it with one hand. The bread keeps sliding away."

"Sure," said Max. She spread peanut butter on two pieces of bread, slapped two more pieces on top. She handed a sandwich to Sophie, taking a bite of her own. "You going to tell them tonight or in the morning?"

"Tomorrow," said Sophie. "I need some time to think about how to say it." She heard Twixie's claws on the floor and looked up to see the big dog trotting out of the kitchen. "They must be here. Twixie probably heard the car turn into the driveway," she said. "They'll be in the house in a minute."

"You have no idea how glad I am you made it back in

85

time," said Max emphatically. "I didn't know what I was going to tell them."

"Quick! What was the movie about?" asked Sophie through a mouthful of peanut butter.

"Kalene phoned before it was halfway through and I told her you were asleep," said Max. "Just tell her it was about mummies and Egyptian curses. It was pretty good. You should watch it sometime."

"I'll tell them that I barely woke up and we decided to have a snack," said Sophie. She turned around. "Oh yeah, can you undo my braid?"

"I'm glad you're going to bring Aria home, Soph," said Max, as she laid her peanut butter sandwich on the countertop. She untied Sophie's braid and shook it loose. "I was thinking about it while you were gone. I didn't see how you could take care of her with a broken arm either. I would have helped, but honestly, I would have felt guilty whenever I was around Joel and Kalene."

"Like I do already. I just hope they can forgive me," said Sophie, in a small voice. She heard the front door open and the murmur of voices come from the front hallway.

"Sure they will," said Max. "I mean, nothing bad happened to Aria. She's fine and she's so pretty that I'm sure that the foal will be gorgeous too, even if it isn't a purebred Arabian. They'll love Melody."

"That's not why I'm afraid to tell them," whispered Sophie, so Kalene and Joel wouldn't hear her. "I'm afraid they'll send me away. I'm afraid they'll think they can never trust me again. I'm just a foster kid, remember? They don't have to keep me."

Max was shocked. "Do you really think they'll send you away?" she asked. "But they can't…" She stopped speaking when she heard Kalene call her name. "We're in the

86

kitchen," she answered, her dark eyes locked onto Sophie's. "They can't send you away," she whispered vehemently just before Joel and Kalene walked into the kitchen.

Sophie swallowed her emotion and turned toward Kalene with a smile. "How was the play?" she asked as brightly as she could.

"It was wonderful," said Kalene enthusiastically. "You would have loved it. I wish you could have come."

"Me too," said Sophie.

"Even I liked it," said Joel. "Just don't get run over the day before next time, and you can come with us."

Sophie tried to smile. *But there won't be a next time,* she thought. *By tomorrow, you won't see me the same way and everything will change.*

When Sophie didn't reply, an uncomfortable silence filled the kitchen. Max came to the rescue. "We had a great time here," she said forcing her voice to sound cheerful. "I watched the movie and Sophie slept."

Joel laughed. "Sounds like a night to remember," he said.

"Sorry to cut all the fun short," said Kalene. "But I promised your mom we'd have you back home by eleven, Max."

Within a couple of minutes, Joel and Kalene left to drive Max home. "Phone me tomorrow," Sophie called to Max as her friend walked out the door.

"I will," replied Max. "As soon as I get home from school."

When they were gone, Sophie went to her room with Twixie right behind her. She knew Joel and Kalene would be back within fifteen minutes and she wanted to be in bed before they returned. Tomorrow morning would be soon enough to talk to them about Aria. There was too much to think about first, like *how* she was going to tell them. Maybe she could find a way to say the words and not make herself sound like such a horrible person.

Within minutes Sophie was in her pajamas. She lay with her hand trailing over the edge of the bed, resting on Twixie's head, and thinking of what to say. It all sounded so awful. Everything made her sound like a thief who had stolen their horse. *I sound exactly like what I am,* she thought sadly.

Sighing, she turned onto her side, facing the wall. *There must be some way to say it. Concentrate,* she commanded herself. But her thoughts kept shifting. To Aria. *So beautiful. So patient.* To Angelica and Sky. *How did she ask him to take me home? And what an amazing ride!* To Melody. *I love her already and I haven't even seen her yet.*

Again she tried concentrating on the conversation she was going to have with Joel and Kalene. *I must have a plan. I need to figure out how to tell them.*

But it was no use. Visions of a beautiful dark filly pranced into her mind. Behind her were Aria and Sky, the proud sire and dam. Like magical beings, they cavorted behind Sophie's eyelids. She pictured the horses trotting through the canyon and galloping across the desert. Then Angelica was there too, astride Sky's powerful back. Her hair looked dark even in the moonlight and in Sophie's thoughts it spread over Sky's back like a silver-blue mantle, blending the two of them into one creature.

Then Sophie thought she heard Angelica whisper, "Sleep now. There is nothing to plan. There is only truth to tell. That is all that must be done."

Sophie's eyes flew open and she looked over her shoulder to peer into the darkness. The voice seemed so real. But the room was still. Tranquil. She heard Twixie's deep breathing as the dog slept on the rug beside her bed. Sophie felt peace gather around and flow over her. She closed her eyes again. Her mind quieted and within seconds, she slipped into a comforting, soothing sleep.

When Joel and Kalene returned home, Sophie didn't notice them come into her room or hear them whisper to each other over her bed. She didn't feel Kalene reach out and touch her hand or, a few minutes later, hear them slip from the room. In her dreams, she was riding Aria. Melody ran beside them like a swift little bird. They were skimming over the desert, following an angel who rode ahead on a blue roan mustang.

Sophie's eyes sprung open. It was morning! And she felt wonderful: whole and energetic. It was as if the sleep she woke from had restored not only her body, but her mind as well. She flexed her arm inside her cast. It still felt fine. *All I needed was a good night's sleep,* thought Sophie. *In my own bed with without any nurses to bug me.*

She sat up and glanced at the clock. Joel would be starting work on the ranch and Kalene would be leaving for her job soon. Sophie took a deep breath. It was time to talk to her foster parents, before Kalene went to work and before Sophie lost her nerve.

Kalene was pouring milk on her cereal when Sophie walked into the kitchen. "How are you feeling this morning, Sophie?" Kalene asked. "How's your arm?"

"It doesn't hurt at all," said Sophie. "It feels totally normal, except it's in a cast and its pretty itchy. I wish I could reach inside to scratch it!"

Kalene raised her eyebrows. "Well, it's good that it doesn't hurt any more," she said, surprised. "I thought it would."

"Me too," agreed Sophie. She reached up in the cupboard to get a bowl, then carefully shook some cereal into it.

"I'll help you with the milk," offered Kalene.

"Thanks," said Sophie as Kalene lifted the milk jug.

When Sophie sprinkled a spoonful of sugar on top of the cereal, Kalene wrinkled her nose. "I don't understand how you can like it even sweeter," she said. "It already seems too sweet to me."

"That's because I'm a kid," said Sophie. "All sweet stuff tastes good to me, remember?"

Kalene laughed. "You're right. I loved sugar on my cereal, and on everything else when I was young. Now it just tastes gross."

Together they walked into the dining room and set their bowls on the table. As Sophie pulled up a chair opposite Kalene, she felt the first twinge of uncertainty. *How am I going to tell them?* She closed her eyes. *How am I even going to start?*

"Sophie? Are you okay?" asked Kalene, her voice filled with concern. "Are you sure your arm isn't hurting? You don't have to be brave you know. If it hurts, just say so."

Sophie opened her eyes. "No, I'm fine" she said and bit her lip. She looked down at her cereal. *Just do it,* she commanded herself. *Just have the guts and do it.* "Kalene? I need to talk to you and Joel," said Sophie in a quiet voice.

Sophie heard Kalene put her spoon down, then she spoke gently to Sophie. "We wanted to talk to you too, Sophie," she said. Sophie was surprised to hear Kalene's voice trembling. "We were going to wait until tonight," continued Kalene. "But I can't wait anymore. I'll go get Joel and then we can all say what we want to say."

Do they know about Aria? Questions catapulted into Sophie's mind. *But how could they? How could they know about the wild stallion and about me falling asleep on the desert? But I don't know what else they would want to talk about.* She shuddered uncontrollably.

Kalene's chair scraped back. Sophie didn't look up, but instead reached out with her good arm and pushed her cereal back. She wasn't hungry any more. If Kalene and Joel knew about Aria, and if Kalene already sounded so stressed, then Sophie knew it wouldn't go well.

But at least Aria will be home and safe, Sophie reminded herself as tears brimmed in her eyes. *I just hope they accept Melody too. It's not her fault that I didn't watch Aria that day. It's not her fault that her sire is a wild stallion instead of Rolly.*

She heard the low murmur of voices as Joel came in from outside and Kalene talked to him in the foyer. Sophie quickly rubbed her eyes on her sleeve and looked up. She hoped they wouldn't be able to tell she had almost cried. Well, maybe a little more than almost.

When Joel came in, his face was serious. Sophie watched him solemnly as he sat across from her at the table. Kalene pulled up a chair to sit beside her.

"So what did you want to talk about?" asked Kalene, gently.

Sophie could tell by Kalene's worried expression that she had noticed the redness in Sophie's eyes. Sophie opened her mouth. "I... I..." she stuttered, but the rest of the words wouldn't come. She looked at her hands and tried to force herself to say something. Anything. Joel and Kalene patiently waited for her to speak.

But if they already know, if somehow they have already found out, why even bother telling them, she thought. *I'll just let them tell me. It'll be easier...* "Why don't you go first," she finally said. The room fell back into silence.

Then Joel cleared his throat. "Sophie," he said. "You've been living with us for just over a year now, right?"

When Sophie nodded, Kalene spoke. "Do you like living here?" she asked.

"Yes," said Sophie clearly, insistently.

Kalene looked at Joel and again, he cleared his throat. Finally he spoke. "I guess there is no easy way to say this Sophie."

Sophie nodded. She knew what was coming next. It

would be hard to hear, especially from Kalene and Joel, but she could take it. She could act tough and pretend it didn't matter and make them think she wanted to go too, just as much as they wanted her to leave.

"When you were struck by the car, Kalene and I knew we had to say something to you. We've wanted to for quite a while now, but just didn't know how." He stopped and looked at his wife. "Your accident scared us. Very badly."

"I don't know if you realize how much you mean to us, Sophie," said Kalene.

"So I'll just say it, Sport. Kalene and I were wondering if you might want to stay with us," said Joel, slowly. "For always." For a moment, his voice faltered. "We were wondering if you wouldn't mind too much if we adopted you."

"What?" exclaimed Sophie, not sure she had heard right. "What did you say?"

"We know it's a hard choice, honey. Really. And we know we can never take the place of your mom, but…" Kalene's voice faded away.

"You want to adopt me?" said Sophie, still unbelieving. "You want to adopt *me*?" She felt a hidden joy begin to bubble up inside of her. *I can't believe it,* she thought as she forced the feeling down. *I must have heard wrong! I must have. Why would they want me? I'm not cool or talented or pretty or anything.*

"Yes, we want to adopt you. In fact there is nothing we would love more than having you for our daughter," said Joel. "But only if that's what you want, too."

Both Kalene and Joel sat silently and waited for Sophie to respond. But Sophie was speechless. A thousand questions raced through her head and none of them seemed to have any answers. How could Kalene and Joel want to adopt her? How could they love her when she was so horrid? And what

93

about her mom? What if she came back? Would she blame Sophie for wanting to be part of a family, a family that wouldn't include her? And what about Kalene and Joel's own children – if and when they ever had any? Would Sophie just be shoved aside when they were born?

Then a single thought rose from the tangled web. *What will they think when I tell them about Aria?*

"You don't have to decide right now," said Kalene softly and Sophie turned to her with stricken eyes. She could see the disappointment on Kalene's face and it made her own pain stronger.

If they knew I had stolen Aria from them, if they knew they couldn't trust me, they wouldn't be asking me to become their daughter, Sophie realized. *They'd be a lot more than just disappointed in me. They'd be angry. How can I tell them about her now? How can I ever let them know about Melody?*

But they don't need to know. I'll think of something. Maybe I can turn Aria loose and she and Melody can both become wild horses. Sky will keep them safe from the mountain lion and Angelica won't be stuck here then. She can go off to save other horses. And if that won't work, I'll have to think of something else, something besides telling Kalene and Joel about Aria. I've never wanted anything as much as I want to be adopted by them. I just never dreamed they would ever want me.

"Joel? Kalene?" said Sophie looking at each of them in turn. "Yes. I want you to adopt me. So much! I want you to be my mom and dad."

Huge grins spread across Joel and Kalene's faces and Kalene laughed with joy. "Oh Sophie," she exclaimed. "You have made me the happiest woman in the world!" She pulled Sophie into a huge hug.

Sophie melted into Kalene's arms. She felt so safe. So warm inside, as if she had finally come home after a long, long journey.

This is where I belong, she thought. She wept tears of happiness as she held fast to Kalene. Then she felt Joel's strong arms go around them both.

"You better stop that crying, Sport," he warned. "Either that, or I'll have to join you."

Sophie couldn't help but laugh through her tears. She couldn't imagine Joel crying. Not for anything. He was the toughest guy she knew. And the perfect dad, the only dad she ever wanted. "Maybe I want to see you cry," she teased him after the hug loosened and she pulled back to look at her new parents.

"Well, I'll tell you, girl," said Joel, gruffly. "You almost saw it. I was more nervous asking you to be our daughter than I was when I asked Kalene to marry me. I figured she would say yes, but I didn't know which way you'd go. I thought there was a pretty good chance you might say no."

"Not a chance," said Sophie, looking from one to the other. "No chance of that. Ever. You're stuck with me now. For as long as you want me."

"For a very, very long time then," said Kalene, brushing tears from her eyes and beaming at Sophie. "We'll be a family for always."

Unwanted thoughts rose up through Sophie's happiness like needles through a balloon. Nagging at her, insisting on being heard. She wanted to hug Kalene again, to be wrapped inside her arms and hidden away from the guilt. She wanted to close her eyes and hear nothing but Joel and Kalene tell her over and over how much they wanted her for their daughter.

"So what did you want to talk to us about?" asked

Kalene. "I hate to hurry you, sweetheart, but I've got to be off to work soon."

"Oh, it was nothing," faltered Sophie. She looked down at her cast. "I… um… just wanted to say… thanks for being so nice to me when I broke my arm. And for taking care of me."

"Well, of course we'd take care of you, honey," said Kalene surprised. "You're our daughter. We've thought of you that way for months now."

"That's right, Sport," said Joel and grinned. "And if we don't get that broken arm feeling better soon, then who am I going to tease? Whenever I bug Kalene, she just hits me. She's no fun."

"Hey," protested Kalene, poking Joel in the arm with her finger. "I don't *hit* you."

"See what I mean, Sophie?" said Joel in an injured voice. "She picks on me all the time."

Sophie smiled at their antics, but she felt she was watching them through a haze. Then Kalene was hugging her one more time and leaving for work and Joel was explaining that he had to go to town for a load of feed, but he'd be back soon.

Sophie said, "No thanks," when he asked if she wanted to come along. She told him she wanted to watch the movie she missed the night before. She acted as normal as she could as the thoughts crashed through her mind. The same questions over and over.

If they knew I had stolen Aria, would they still want me? Would they still love me?

Beautiful, beautiful Melody! Jumping and leaping about, testing her legs. And such long legs!

She is so curious. She sees everything with those bright eyes. Now she is trying to sneak up on a sparrow. She is much like Aria in physical form and much like Sky in color and gait, but in personality she is completely herself. Mischievous, inquisitive, loving, and fun.

The morning sun is glorious. I am so glad this night is over. Now I can rest. I am sure the lion has gone back to his den. I hope he will stay there and not return until tonight. Aria and Melody should be back home in their own barn by then, safe and secure. He will find only an empty corral.

Did the bird fly away, Melody? What are you going to do now? Oh. You want to play with me? How can I refuse such a delightful offer? Of course I will play with you!

As soon as she could, Sophie went to her room. Twixie moped along behind her, copying Sophie's dejected walk. The dog pushed her muzzle into Sophie's hands as soon as she sat on the bed.

"I don't know what I'm going to do," said Sophie, stroking the big black head for a moment. "Oh Twixie. What would you do if you were me?"

She pulled her knees up and hugged them to her chest. Twixie stared at her with sad eyes. "Everything is so complicated. I wish none of this had happened," continued Sophie. "Why did I fall asleep that day? I normally don't do things like that. And why did the wild herd have to be there? If none of this had happened, if Aria wasn't in foal to a mustang, and if it all wasn't my fault, I would be so happy now. So happy…" her voice trailed away and tears came to her eyes.

There was a knock on her door. "Sophie?" called Joel. "I'm heading into town now. Are you sure you don't want to come?"

"I'm sure," said Sophie, quickly. "I… I think I might rest for a while instead of watching the movie."

"You feeling okay?" Joel called through the door. Sophie knew he wouldn't come in unless she invited him. At least, he never had before.

"Yeah, I'm okay," she said. "Just tired."

"I've got a couple other errands to run too, so I'll probably be gone for a while, okay?"

"Okay," said Sophie, wishing he would just hurry and go. She was feeling worse and worse, listening to the concern in his voice. When she heard the front door shut behind him, Sophie stood up and went to the window. She watched him walk to the truck and climb inside. When he drove out the driveway, she exhaled, not even realizing she had been holding her breath.

"Time to go," Sophie whispered to Twixie and wiped the last of the tears from her eyes. Twixie leapt to her feet with her tail whipping back and forth. "Oh, sorry Twix. Time for me to go. You have to stay," she added. "If Sky is there, I don't want him to kick you or anything. I don't think wild horses like dogs any more than they like mountain lions." She rubbed Twixie's ears and the big black dog stretched her head out, then whipped around so that Sophie could scratch the top of her behind.

Sophie patted Twixie on her rump. "You're a funny girl, Twix," she said. "I wish you could come. I could use the company right now. I feel so horrible."

Within a few minutes, Sophie was out the back door. As she walked across the pasture, her eyes searched the desert. Sky was nowhere in sight. Sophie sighed. She thought it had been too much to hope for to have the wild stallion give her a ride back to the canyon, but it would have been nice.

But it won't be too hard to get there today. My arm doesn't hurt any more and I don't have anything to carry. Not like last night, thought Sophie as she climbed through the fence and walked among the sagebrush. Then she broke into a jog.

Birds cavorted around her as she ran, flying from bush to bush, collecting nesting material. Their twittering filled the air and a soft morning breeze cooled Sophie's forehead. Spring was creeping back into the desert. The brown vegeta-

100

tion was turning a subtle green and the air was warm and bright.

But Sophie hardly noticed. She kept her eyes fastened on the ground and occasionally glanced up at the hills growing larger in front of her. Black clouds perched over the mountains that loomed behind, and she could hear faint rumbling in the distance, ominous and threatening.

The dark skies ahead reflected her mood. After the most magical night she'd ever known had come the happiest morning. Until the guilt came crashing in. The guilt of planning to leave Aria to have her foal with the wild ones. The guilt of stealing the mare from Joel and Kalene. It had been different before. She always expected to return the mare, so it hadn't seemed like she was *really* stealing, only borrowing. But if she turned Aria out with the mustangs, she would definitely have stolen her. For real. She, Sophie, would be a thief. But not just any thief. She would be a thief that stole from those who loved and trusted her. She would be the worst kind of thief there is.

Sophie ran faster. Harder. She leapt over the smaller sagebrush instead of running around, her feet pounding in rhythm with her breath. In rhythm with her heart. She ran faster and faster, trying to outrun the choice she knew she must make. She ran from the vision of the family she could have belonged to. The perfect family. She would always think of Joel and Kalene as her real parents – not the mom who had walked out on her – not any of the other foster parents. Whenever she thought of family, parents, a place of belonging, it would be Joel and Kalene's faces that she would see.

Slowly, Sophie came to a stop and sank to the ground. She covered her face with her hand. She knew there was only one way to make Aria and Melody safe. One way to

101

help Kalene and Joel get their most valuable mare back. There was only one way to show them she loved them. She had to tell them the truth. And when she told them they would know how careless she had been with Aria's safety last year. They would know that Aria was going to give birth to a foal that wasn't a purebred Arab.

But that's not even the bad stuff. Those things were just mistakes. They probably wouldn't have blamed me too much if I had told them about it right away, she finally realized. *They would have been disappointed in me, but not too angry. But how can they forgive me for what I've done since? How can they forgive me when I tell them that I stole Aria away, when I explain how I put her in danger, when they know how I've lied to them all these months? Instead of forgiving, they'll see what my mom saw all those years ago. They'll see that I'm a bad person. They'll see that all I'll do is poison their home. And then they'll send me away.*

Sophie's eyes stung as the tears flowed. There was no point in trying to run. There was no way she could run from what she knew to be true. If she was to do the right thing, she would have to return Aria. The mare belonged with Kalene and Joel. And so did all her future foals.

I might as well face it, I'm just not good enough for them, Sophie thought as she looked toward the distant mountains. *They would have found that out sooner or later anyway. Maybe it's better for them to send me away now, before I start to love them too much.*

Slowly, she climbed to her feet and walked toward the mouth of the main canyon. *But it's too late for that. Much too late. I already do.*

The mountain lion couldn't sleep. He lay his head on his forepaws, flexing his muscles and twitching his tail. His power was returning, his strength building in fierce, unrelenting waves, fed by his hatred and revulsion of the Bright Creature. He kept seeing the creature in his mind. It hadn't looked strong physically, and he wondered now if it was. Maybe the only thing powerful about it was its light, its goodness. And there had only been that one flash of light. Once its light went forth, was the Bright Creature without power for a time? And if it was, for how long? Long enough for his teeth to sink into its neck? Long enough for him to taste its blood? The lion growled and stared into the darkness of the crevice.

Did it have any other powers? Powers like his own? Like his strongest ally: hatred? If not, it was limited. If it didn't hate, if it was only concerned with good and right, he would have an advantage. It wouldn't understand the depths of his consuming desire to see it dead. It wouldn't know the lengths to which he would go to kill it.

But most of all, if the Bright Creature was only concerned with good, it wouldn't be concentrating on hurting him. It would only be concerned with protecting the others. In that would lie his biggest advantage. The Bright Creature wouldn't know that he didn't care about killing the others. It would make the mistake of trying to protect them. It might even want to sacrifice itself for them and in doing that, would fall right into the lion's trap. He could kill the others afterward, at his leisure, if he wanted. If killing the Bright Creature wasn't satisfying enough for him.

The mountain lion knew the Bright Creature would be ready for him tonight. But would it expect him during the day? Rising from his rocky bed in the crevice, he skulked toward the sunlit ledge. He could wait no more. The opportunity was now. The attack would be a surprise.

The greatest hunt of his life had begun. He would bring down the Bright Creature if it was the last thing he ever did.

Now that she knew what she had to do, Sophie was determined to carry out her decision. She swallowed her despair as best she could and walked resolutely toward the canyon, striding forward in an effort to look and feel confident. She *would* do the right thing: she *would* return Aria. She would make sure the mare was safe, and that the foal was born and brought up in a good home. She would free Angelica from her obligation to protect the mare so she could go to other horses that needed help. Then she would confess everything to Kalene and Joel. No matter what, no matter how much it hurt, she would do the right thing. She wouldn't burden them with a daughter like her. She would tell them how horrible she really was.

And then I want to forget about Aria and Sky and Angelica and Melody, she thought. *I want to forget about the magical night that was followed by the perfect morning. I have to forget them all, especially Kalene and Joel, or I'll go crazy.*

When she finally walked into the main canyon, she felt as if the weight of all that stone was heaped on her thin shoulders. She stumbled on a loose rock and automatically tried to save herself with her arms as she fell forward, but the cast didn't allow her right arm to extend and she landed heavily on her side.

"Stupid cast," she said, tears catching at her voice as she pushed her body from the ground and stood. "I'm sure the

105

doctors were wrong. There's no way my arm is broken." She turned her left palm upward to inspect it. It was dusty and scraped. A bit of blood oozed from one of the marks.

"I'll ask Angelica to cut the cast off with my knife," she thought aloud. "Joel and Kalene probably won't even notice it's gone after I tell them about Aria."

Within a few minutes, Sophie was walking into Aria's canyon. When she reached the willow thicket, she slowed her step and trailed her hand along the willow twigs that lined the trail. Too soon she was at the gate. She stopped and took a deep breath.

Just get it over with, she commanded herself, ducking down to slip through the hole. She stood on the other side and looked around for Aria and Angelica.

But what she saw in the middle of the enclosure made her forget everything else. She didn't hear the distant roll of thunder, rumbling through the mountains, louder and deeper than before. She didn't notice that all birdsong was quiet. Standing close to Aria's side was the most perfect foal Sophie had seen in her life. The foal's head and legs were almost black, while the rest of her body was a deep, blue roan. The only white on her body was a thin streak that ran down her nose and ended in a dot, just like an exclamation mark. The foal was looking at Sophie with her finely etched head held high. Her neck and legs were long and her back was short. Her croup was almost tabletop flat, just like Aria's, and her short, soft baby tail was held high. Even Sophie, who had only been around horses for a year, could tell the filly was exceptional.

A high-pitched baby neigh floated toward her. "Hello Melody," she said in a singsong voice. When the filly neighed back to her, Sophie laughed incredulously. The filly was talking to her.

106

"Is she not wonderful?" Angelica asked from the side.

Sophie turned to look at the golden girl leaning against a rock at the edge of the corral. "She's incredible!" breathed Sophie and looked back at Melody. "She's totally amazing!"

"She is a lot like her dam," said Angelica. She moved to stand at Sophie's side. "But she is like her sire, too."

"But he looked so rough and shaggy," said Sophie.

Angelica laughed, her voice chiming sweet and harmonious like soft bells. She tossed her hair back. "He is a Spanish Mustang. Have you ever seen an Andalusian horse?" she asked.

"Yes," said Sophie. "On TV."

"Both the Spanish Mustang and the Andalusian are from the same stock," explained Angelica. "If Sky was pampered and groomed and fed grain, he would look more impressive than many domestic horses."

"And he's Melody's sire," said Sophie in awe. "I'm glad."

"Come and meet her," offered Angelica.

"Will she let me come near her? I don't want to scare her," said Sophie, hanging back though her feet ached to carry her to the foal. "Aren't foals frightened of strangers?"

"I told Melody you would be here soon," said Angelica. "She has been looking forward to meeting you."

Sophie held her hand out in front of her as she drew nearer to the filly and her eyes searched for any sign of fear, but there was none. Instead, when they were close enough, Melody reached toward her, nostrils flaring as she inhaled the girl's scent. Melody's soft nose felt like warm velvet on Sophie's fingers as the filly touched her. The tiny muzzle traveled up Sophie's arm, sniffing, her eyes exploring Sophie's body.

Then their eyes fastened onto each other's. Sophie

108

gasped. She couldn't help herself. It was as if a thin cord of electricity was connecting them, as if she could understand Melody somehow. It wasn't like talking. It was much more subtle than that, but the connection was real. Sophie could see there was a something very special about this filly. She blinked and looked deeper into the liquid brown eyes. *It's as if I can see her spirit shining, strong and gentle.*

"You're amazing," whispered Sophie. "Perfect in every way." She stroked the filly's neck with a feather touch. The wavy baby hair under her fingers was soft and sleek and Sophie loved the way the filly's coat glistened in the sun.

When Melody whinnied to her again, this time a soft, squeaky nicker, Sophie smiled. "It's nice to meet you too, Melody," she replied. "I've been waiting so long! And now that you're here I can see my plan never would have worked. How could I turn you out to be chased by a crazed mountain lion? And without your dam to take care of you? That would be too hard of a life." She moved her hand along the filly's back. "No," she said quietly. "You belong with Kalene and Joel. I just wish you would belong with me, too."

For a moment, Sophie allowed the wonder of Melody to overtake her. What if the filly was hers? What if they could be together forever? Like butterflies of light, the magical thoughts rose and fell and swirled around her.

"She can belong with you. You are taking her home today," said Angelica softly at her side and Sophie felt the lovely floating feeling crash to the ground.

Melody will never belong to me. I might as well face it, she thought. *But at least I know the decision I made is the right one. Melody deserves the best and I will give it to her. Taking her home may be the only thing I can ever do for her, but it'll be the best thing I could ever do.*

"She's so beautiful," Sophie said, knowing she was repeating herself. "It's more than just the way she looks. She's beautiful in her heart. I know I sound crazy, but..."

"No," said Angelica. "You do not sound crazy. There is more to her than her physical beauty. Much, much more."

Abruptly, Sophie pulled her fingers from Melody's side and walked away. Her face burned as she strode toward the canyon wall. She bent for a moment at the pool and splashed the cold water on her face, then glanced back at Angelica, Melody, and Aria. Melody was nursing and Aria stared off into space, contented and relaxed. Only Angelica seemed concerned. Her sad eyes were fixed on Sophie. Sophie wanted to tell her that everything was okay, that she wasn't having second thoughts about taking Melody home, but she knew she wouldn't be able to speak. Not yet. Maybe not ever.

Sophie turned, walked to the far side of the small pool, and stepped into the cool darkness of the crevice. A wooden box was sitting on a natural shelf in the rock. Sophie pulled a knife from the box and walked back to the older girl.

"Angelica?" she asked in a tightly controlled voice. "Can you cut away my cast?" She held the knife handle toward Angelica.

Angelica nodded. "There is no need for it any more," she said and took the knife into her hand.

"So you know my arm isn't broken?" Sophie asked, amazed.

"Yes, I could tell when my light passed through you to the mountain lion," said Angelica quietly. "I felt it heal you."

"So that's what happened," Sophie breathed. "You really are magic."

Angelica laughed softly. "No Sophie, I am not magic. I

110

am just different from you. No better and no worse. No stronger or weaker. Just different. My differences are a gift to me, just like your differences are a gift to you. My light allows me to help those I love: the horses – sometimes people." She lowered her head over Sophie's cast with the knife in her hand.

"It must be wonderful, going around helping horses all the time," said Sophie. She looked over Angelica's golden head and tried not to tense her muscles.

"It is wonderful," said Angelica. "Because it is what I was meant to do. All creatures have a purpose. I found mine when I was given the chance to help horses."

Sophie felt the cool air against her right arm and looked down. "How did you do it so fast?" she asked, amazed. "You didn't have time to cut it off. Hey, you said you weren't magic."

"I am not magic," laughed Angelica as she pulled the cast away from Sophie's arm. "Not really. I know it seems that way but that is just because you do not know how some things can be done. Do not feel bad. Most people do not understand many of the forces in this world. Most cannot see the beautiful life they can create."

Sophie couldn't stop staring at Angelica. Slowly she flexed her right arm. How could Angelica have this strange power and then say it wasn't even magic. What else could it be?

I don't care what Angelica says, decided Sophie. *She is magic. There's no other explanation.*

He is here. Suddenly I can feel him, like a black cloud that creeps across the sun. He is watching us, preparing himself to attack.

Why did he not wait until evening? Could he hate us that much? Is he insane?

Or both?

We must go. Now. First I must get Aria and Melody and Sophie away from these bluffs and rocks. There are too many places for him to ambush us from in these canyons. We will be much safer on the desert.

The mountain lion spotted the Bright Creature below. He was sure it hadn't seen him or smelled him. He had used all his skill as a hunter in approaching the lip of the canyon and had come from downwind. Yet he could tell it had sensed him. Although it seemed to focus on the others, the human and the two horses, he felt its consciousness searching for him, probing into the shadows, looking behind rocks.

The lion wasn't worried. The Bright Creature was searching the wrong side of the canyon. Its consciousness probed the side he had attacked from the night before. By the time it finished searching the far side of the canyon and skipped to the side where he now crouched, he would be gone. He would be lying in ambush, waiting for them to pass beneath.

Just before he pulled back over the edge of the canyon, the lion looked more closely at the others. He was glad the mare had foaled. Now there were four of them. The lion licked his lips. After he killed the Bright Creature, he would take them all down. One by one. They would not leave the canyons alive.

"We must go," said Angelica abruptly. "The mountain lion is here. There is not much time. We must get to the desert."

Sophie shook her head. "What? I thought he'd wait until night to attack. I thought we were safe during the day." She spun around to face the canyon wall Angelica was staring at. "We can't let anything happen to Aria or Melody. We have to keep them safe."

"Yes, and we will. It is time to take them home," said Angelica. "You ride Aria in front and Melody will follow. I will come last."

Sophie ran back to the box and pulled out Aria's bridle. Within seconds, it was on the mare's head. Angelica was right. They would be much safer on the desert. On the flat land, they could see the lion coming. Angelica boosted Sophie onto Aria's back and then she untied the ropes and pulled the gate back. Sophie encouraged Aria to walk through onto the willow-lined path leading down to the main canyon. She could hear the creek bubbling and rushing off to the side. A puzzled look crossed her face. The creek sounded louder than usual. She cast her mind back, trying to recall what the pool had looked like when she had bent over it, but she couldn't remember if it was muddier than normal. She had been too upset to pay attention to how stirred up the water might be or if it was higher than usual.

"Does the creek sound louder to you?" she called back to Angelica.

"Yes," the older girl replied. "I think it is because there is much rain in the mountains."

Suddenly, Sophie remembered the thunder she had heard earlier that morning and the black clouds perched over the mountains like an ominous bird. "I hope the big canyon is safe," she said to Angelica. "We have to make sure before we go down. It's one of the major channels out of the mountains and there might be water in it."

There was no reply and she looked behind her. Melody was following, close on Aria's heals, but Angelica had stopped. Her amber eyes were searching the canyon rim. Sophie reined Aria to a halt and watched as Angelica shut her eyes. She stood for a full minute, eyes closed, perfectly still. Then her eyes suddenly opened.

"He is ahead of us," she said to Sophie in an urgent whisper. "He waits in the narrowest part of Aria's canyon, where it meets the larger one. He wants us to pass beneath him."

"What do we do?" Sophie whispered back, trying to keep the panic from her voice. There was only one way out and if the lion was guarding it, how would they escape? They could take Aria and Melody back to the enclosure, but that wouldn't be any safer. The lion could easily get close enough to them, under the cover of the willow bushes, to attack. Melody was especially vulnerable. Sophie couldn't bear the thought of anything happening to her.

"Is there another way out of the canyon?" Angelica asked quietly.

"I don't think so," answered Sophie, wishing she had more to add to the sentence. An alternate plan. Another escape route. She turned Aria around so that she was facing Angelica.

"Let me think for a minute," said Angelica.

All Sophie could see was how effectively the mountain

lion had trapped them. She knew there was no way they could get past him. The entrance to Aria's canyon was narrow and the rocks were high. It would be easy for the predator to wait until they walked beneath him and then leap on one of them. The lion could be immediately fatal to herself or Melody. Aria might be able to shake it off, although Sophie doubted it. The mare was weakened from giving birth and any horse was at a disadvantage against a mountain lion's teeth and claws. Angelica could not, or would not, hurt the lion. She could possibly frighten it away or maybe throw it from them with her light. Or try to change its mind, try to convince it to leave them alone.

But it has already made its choice, Sophie realized. *It wants to kill us all.*

"What if we run as fast as we can through the opening?" she said, but as soon as the words came out of her mouth, she knew it wouldn't work. Aria could run fast, but Melody wouldn't be as quick. Could she outrun a mountain lion? And even if she could, Angelica wouldn't be able to. "No, we can't do that," she said before Angelica could agree. *It would be just like her to sacrifice herself to the lion so we could get away,* thought Sophie.

"Could we use Sky to distract the mountain lion?" asked Sophie, her voice brightening. "Maybe he could lead it away from us."

"It is us that the lion wants," Angelica replied. "Otherwise he would not have returned after I frightened him last night. He would seek easier prey."

Sophie fell silent and looked down at Aria's mane. Her fingers absently played with the silky, silver hair, twirling a single strand around and around. In her mind, she was checking every part of the small canyon they were standing in. Were all the walls too steep for a horse to climb? Or was

116

there a way somewhere? Even a narrow deer trail would be better than nothing.

Then, suddenly, she remembered. There *was* another way out of the canyon. The crevice behind Aria's corral, the cave-like opening behind the pool, led to a trail high up on the main canyon wall. A narrow trail snaked from the end of the crevice to the canyon below, rocky, steep and dangerous. It was a deer trail and Sophie doubted that anything as big as a horse had ever traveled it before. But it was another way out.

Sophie had explored most of the crevice on foot when she prepared the hidden corral for Aria. Thinking Aria might try to leave the canyon, Sophie had blocked it off with some of the willow bushes she'd cut from the enclosure. Once Aria's belly became larger with Melody growing inside of her, Sophie stopped worrying about her slipping out of the enclosure. The passageway was too narrow for a pregnant mare. But with Melody born, Aria would be thin enough again.

Sophie took a deep breath. "There is another way," she said to Angelica and crossed her fingers. They all just had to make it out safely.

Within a few minutes, the four were back inside the corral. While Angelica stood guard, Sophie pulled the dead willows out of the crevice and piled them to the side. When the way was clear, Sophie called Angelica. Angelica walked around the pool, watching the footing, making sure it was safe for Aria and Melody. The two horses followed close behind.

Upon reaching Sophie, Angelica turned to remove the bridle from Aria's head. "I do not want her to get tangled in the reins," she explained to Sophie. "Even if they are tied on her neck, there is a chance they might slip to the side causing her to trip. We cannot take that chance since the way ahead is dangerous."

"Should I carry it?" asked Sophie.

"No, we will leave it," replied Angelica. She smiled at Sophie. "Aria will let you ride her without it. And she knows her way home." Angelica turned toward Aria and stood on tiptoes. Then she whispered in Aria's ear. Though Sophie tried to listen, she only heard the wind, sliding through the crevice and sighing around her.

"What did you tell her?" asked Sophie when Angelica pulled away from Aria.

"I told her to take you and Melody to safety no matter what happens," replied Angelica.

"But I'm responsible for Aria and Melody's safety," said

118

Sophie. "It's up to me to get them home safe. I brought them here."

"You *are* responsible for Aria and Melody, but Aria has also accepted responsibility for you," said Angelica. "It is the way things should be. All beings caring for each other."

Sophie nodded and looked into Aria's dark eyes. The mare gazed back at her with a warm, almost motherly expression. Sophie put out her hand and touched the silver neck. She had no doubt that Aria would take care of her. Then Sophie's forehead creased. "But shouldn't we be responsible for you too, then?" she asked Angelica. "Shouldn't we make sure you are safe?"

Angelica looked at her with surprised eyes. "We must go," she said after a moment. "The mountain lion will soon get suspicious that we have found another way."

"But Angelica, I mean it. We will keep you safe…" Sophie's voice trailed away. Rainbow dewdrops glistened in Angelica's tawny eyes.

"Very few people have shown such concern for me," she said to Sophie and reached up to wipe her tears. "You amaze me, Sophie. The horses care for me, but humans usually think I am here only to look after them. Few worry about me. You are very special, Sophie."

In the silence that followed her words, Sophie felt her heart swelling. Was she really special, as Angelica had said? She always felt so worthless. So expendable. Somewhere deep inside her she felt a tiny hope start to grow: maybe there was something good about her after all. Maybe. "Come," Angelica urged. "You lead the way. Aria, then Melody can follow. I will come down the trail last. Try to be as quiet as you can."

Sophie picked her way carefully into the crevice, being sure to take care so Aria and Melody wouldn't feel pres-

119

sured to hurry. Though not much could happen to them in the narrow crevice, they had to get used to picking their way through the rocks. If they slipped on the trail and fell, they could be killed. The rock walls were so close that being in the crevice was almost like being in a cave, except there was a bit of blue sky above them. Sophie looked up. If the mountain lion knew they were coming this way and leapt from above, they wouldn't stand a chance. There was no room to dart to the side, and they couldn't run forward because of the cliff in front of them.

We would have to back out, realized Sophie. *With a mountain lion attacking us, it wouldn't be possible. I hope Angelica is right and the mountain lion is at the other end of Aria's canyon.*

After one more fearful glance upward, Sophie walked faster keeping an eye out for rattlesnakes as she went. The mid-morning sun was heating up the rock walls and trail and Sophie knew any creatures out in the sun would be thinking about the cool refreshing shade inside the crevice.

The ground began to rise and Sophie climbed upward. Then the floor sharply descended. Sophie could hear Aria sliding behind her, her hooves scrambling over the loose stones. They turned a last corner in the crevice and she could see the far wall of the main canyon through the narrow channel. Then Sophie was at the mouth of the crevice. She stepped out onto the trail. Aria nickered behind her.

Sophie had forgotten how high the crevice was above the main canyon floor and looked in dismay at the trail they had to follow. It didn't look very safe. It was steep and rocky and a portion of it had been swept away in a rock slide.

She was relieved to see that the canyon below didn't have water in it – yet. It was obviously still raining in the mountains. The clouds that hung over the distant spires were

heavy and dark even though it was still hot and sunny in the canyon. Sophie could see distant thunderheads dumping their burden of rain.

She glanced over the edge of the trail and a wave of dizziness washed over her. Quickly she pulled back and closed her eyes. The air around her was heavy and suffocating.

Sophie turned back to Aria. "I'll do everything I can to get you and Melody down safe, Aria," she whispered and leaned her head against the mare's forehead. "If I didn't have you to protect, I don't know if I could do this." Aria stood calmly and Sophie shut her eyes again and soaked in the quiet presence of the horse. Finally she pulled away.

With a quickly-beating heart Sophie turned to face the rocky incline. "Let's go, Aria," she whispered and took her first step.

The mountain lion is still waiting at the mouth of Aria's canyon, but he is becoming suspicious. He is unsure that his plan of attack is the best one. He heard us coming down Aria's canyon and now wonders why he can no longer hear our voices or our movement. He does not know there is another way but soon he will come to look for us. If we are lucky, we will be in the main canyon by then, already racing for the desert.

And once we are on the desert, Aria will follow her instructions. She will gallop to safety with Sophie on her back and Melody racing behind her. She has promised to leave me if she has to. She wants the same thing I do: she wants Melody and Sophie to be safe.

But first we must make it to the floor of the main canyon. The mountain lion must not catch us on the cliff-side trail. Yet one slip, one missed step, and any one of us could fall to our death.

Sophie found the going relatively easy at first. The ground wasn't too steep and the trail was wide enough for the horses. But Aria would have to descend slowly, and make her way carefully. Though she was a slight horse, she was still a lot bigger than the small desert deer that had carved out the trail. Sophie went slowly downward, pushing rocks and small boulders to the upper side of the path so the horses wouldn't accidentally send any small stones over the edge. The last thing they needed to do was start a rockslide.

Almost a third of the way down, Sophie came to the part that had been ripped away by the rockslide. Since the trail had slid away, the deer had begun wearing a path into the hillside but it was sloped toward the canyon floor and was strewn with loose stones. And there was still one short section that was completely gone. It looked as if the deer had just jumped over that part, not being able to find good enough footing on the ground.

Sophie put her hand back and touched Aria's nose. "Stay here, girl," she whispered. Then, using both her hands and feet, she climbed out onto the new trail.

"We can make it much safer," said Angelica and Sophie looked up to see the older girl edge around the two horses. She picked up a sharp rock and dug at the slope in an effort to widen the new trail. Sophie followed her lead and began to chip at the stones and dirt. Carefully they packed the dirt they had loosened at the side of the trail to stop any stones from tumbling down the hill. More quickly than Sophie thought possible, the short section of trail was dug out. There was only the one gap they couldn't fix.

"Do you think Melody can jump over the part that's missing?" asked Sophie.

"Yes," replied Angelica. "She is small and light enough that she should have no trouble. Aria is going to have more difficulty."

"We can't let her jump it then," said Sophie.

"We have no choice, Sophie. We cannot go back," said Angelica and met the frightened girl's eyes. "The mountain lion is waiting for us. And besides, Aria cannot turn around. The trail is too narrow. We can only go forward. You must be strong and calm no matter what happens. That will help Aria more than anything." Angelica touched Sophie's hand for a second before turning away and squeezing past the two horses again.

"Listen, Aria," said Sophie. "You be careful. You *have* to be careful. You have a daughter to raise, so you can't let anything bad happen. And you've got to get home to Kalene and Joel. I promised I would return you, so be super careful."

She gave Aria's neck one more stroke, then turned to the new trail. Slowly, she walked out onto it. When she reached the gap she jumped as far as she could toward the old, well-worn hillside trail. She landed well onto the hard surface and looked back.

"Okay, Aria," she said. "It's your turn. You can do it. Just take it slow and easy." Sophie backed a few steps away from the gap and waited. The gray mare sniffed at the new trail. She put her front hoof out and tested the ground, slowly shifting her weight. She took another step and another. Sophie felt her heart beat faster as Aria approached. Now

125

she just had to jump over the gap and she would be past the tricky part. "Aria, you can do it," she called encouragingly and backed a few steps to give the horse more room to land. She watched the mare carefully gather herself to jump, then almost in slow motion Aria floated over the gap in the trail.

"Beautiful! That was beautiful! You're amazing," said Sophie and rushed forward to stroke the mare. Aria nickered softly in reply, then looked back at Melody. She nickered again.

Melody came over the new trail like Sophie imagined a deer would, light and quick. Within seconds, she was on the other side, peeking at Sophie from behind her dam. Then Angelica was there as well.

"That was a lot easier than I thought it would be," said Sophie. Her voice was filled with relief. Then she turned to lead them the rest of the way down.

They were close to the bottom when they came to the rock. It was almost as tall and thin as Sophie, and it was leaning against the side of the incline. Sophie knew she could squeeze around it, even though she would be close to the edge of the trail, but Aria wouldn't be able to. But there was something else about this rock that made Sophie nervous. It looked like a snake rock.

Living on the desert for a year had taught Sophie to recognize the places that snakes liked to rest when they were looking for warmth or shade. The rock was big, so it would keep the coolness it had acquired during the night until the next afternoon and the earthy lair between the rock and the canyon wall looked like the ultimate snake hangout.

Sophie called to Angelica. "Can you keep Aria back?" she asked. "I need to make sure its safe."

"What is it?" asked Angelica. She peered around the two horses, her eyes searching the trail in front of Sophie.

"A big rock that looks like a place where snakes would rest," said Sophie. She saw Angelica glance quickly behind them, back toward the crevice that led to Aria's canyon. There was no need for her to tell Sophie to hurry. The mountain lion could come into view at any time, and he was a lot more dangerous than a few sleepy rattlesnakes.

Cautiously, Sophie stepped forward. She wished she had brought a stick with her. She kicked some dirt into the shadow behind the rock. There was no sound, no rustle of movement, no buzz of rattles. *Maybe I'm wrong,* Sophie thought hopefully. She picked up a stone and lobbed it toward the dark hole behind the rock. Still nothing.

Sophie walked as quietly as she could to the boulder, then picked up another larger rock and tapped loudly on the big one. Sharp hammering filled the air, and still there was no response. Not even a whisper of movement.

It must be okay, thought Sophie, as she walked beside the rock and looked on the other side.

All she saw was a blur of movement flash toward her, quick as a tongue of lightening. Instinctively, Sophie threw herself backward on the trail, leaving the snake to snap its jaws just an inch from her leg. Her heart thumped so hard she thought it would explode as she scrambled backward in the dust. Sophie was lucky she hadn't fallen over the edge of the trail. She jumped to her feet and hurried back toward Aria.

Then she stopped. There was only one way to make the way safe for the others. Only one way to widen the trail. *And I better just do it. I can't stop to think, or I'll chicken out!*

With a quick step, Sophie was back at the boulder. Her eyes watched the bottom of the large rock for movement as she leaned into it and pushed with all her might.

127

The rock was precariously balanced, thinner at the base than at the top. Slowly, slowly, it scraped along the side of the cliff, loosening dust and small stones. As gravity caught it, it fell faster. Sophie hoped that the snake would be able to get out of the way. As long as it left them alone, she didn't want to kill it.

The boulder hit the trail with a loud crash, then heavily rolled for a few feet before it toppled over the edge. Sophie was relieved to see that the snake was okay. It slithered away in panic with another right behind it. They whipped over the edge of the trail and disappeared among the rocks on the steep slope. When they disappeared in the dust caused by the falling rock, Sophie breathed a sigh of relief.

At least they're not hurt, she thought. *The snake didn't mean to scare me. I just startled it.*

Suddenly her thoughts of snakes stopped short. She had just realized something terrible about the loud crashing noise the boulder made as it tumbled down the slope, loosening the smaller rocks that bounced and clattered and echoed along behind it. It was much too loud.

The lion will hear it, Sophie thought and her stomach suddenly felt queasy. *He might have been around the corner, waiting for us at the other end of Aria's canyon, but he heard that. He'll be coming now.*

He heard the rock slide.
 He knows we have taken too long to pass beneath him.
 He knows we have found another way.

"Go! Hurry," Angelica yelled behind Sophie.

Sophie quickened her pace, but she didn't dare go faster than a rapid walk. As it was she could hear Aria behind her, hooves skidding on the steep slope.

Sophie quickly pushed another large rock out of the way to make Aria and Melody's path a bit easier. There was no point in being quiet now. The lion would be coming. Sophie shuddered despite the heat shimmering around her.

As the trail widened at the bottom, she walked faster and finally ran the last few steps down to the canyon floor. Here it was bare of everything but rock and sand. No willow surrounded the new trickle of muddy water that ran between the rock walls. Sophie stopped and turned back.

"Where is he?" she asked Angelica. "Can you tell? Is he coming down the trail after us or will he wait somewhere up high and attack as we pass beneath?"

Angelica's face tightened in concentration. She closed her eyes. Sophie could feel her reaching out, not with her hands, but with something that couldn't be seen. Something that felt like fingers of energy probing and searching.

"He is above us. Maybe in Aria's enclosure. It is hard to tell exactly," the golden girl finally said. "But we cannot wait to find out. We must go quickly. If he is in the enclosure, he will be here shortly. We can move faster if you ride Aria."

Angelica boosted Sophie onto Aria's back and the mare

130

immediately trotted toward the open desert. Melody loped behind her dam and Angelica brought up the rear, running quickly over the rough ground.

Most of the trail was covered with the brown water, so the going was slower than it otherwise would have been. They had to move at a pace the horses could easily handle and Melody, especially, was having trouble. She was only a few hours old, and already she'd had to negotiate rocky, uneven ground.

Rounding the corner, Sophie guided Aria with her heels as far away from the entrance to Aria's hidden canyon as she could, while keeping an eye on the narrow opening to her left. There seemed to be no movement. *Maybe the mountain lion is in Aria's corral, searching for us,* she thought. *Or maybe he's heading down the deer trail right now. If so, we'll get to the desert before he catches us.*

She glanced back at Angelica. The older girl was keeping up behind Melody. She didn't look tired at all. Her long golden hair streamed out behind her like a molten cape, flashing in the morning sun. Ahead, Sophie could see the desert between the canyon walls, its dry expanse stretching away to the horizon.

We're almost there, she realized. *We've almost made it.* She urged Aria on a little faster. They were so close. So close.

The mountain lion watched the horses and the girl trot by him. Then the Bright Creature ran past. He was right to come back to the entrance to the smaller canyon. His attack would still be a surprise. He had stayed down low this time instead of climbing on top of the rocks at the entrance.

Sliding out from the shadows, he ran swiftly behind the Bright Creature. A dozen different ways to attack flashed through his mind. Different ways to kill.

Then the Bright Creature stopped. It looked at him as if it knew he was there all along. A worthy adversary.

At last he would have satisfaction.

There he is. No more running. I will face him for I am the one he
wants. I can see that now.

At all costs, Aria and Melody and Sophie must be kept safe.

Here I am, lion. Come to me.

I offer myself to you.

Come.

When Sophie saw the large boulders ahead, she directed Aria with her legs to the trail close to the creek.

It was then that she noticed a brown wave wash down the creek beside her, about two feet high and racing along faster than they were cantering. She looked at it with a puzzled expression.

"Whoa, Aria," she called and looked back. Angelica wasn't following them. She was farther up the creek, facing back the way they had come. Sophie saw another brown, swollen wave of water wash toward the girl.

"Angelica," she yelled. "These are just the first waves! It's probably a flash flood! We've got to get out of here!"

Angelica turned and stared at Sophie for a few seconds, then shook her head. The wave of water washed past her, carving the channel in the center of the canyon even deeper.

"Angelica, you have to come now!" Sophie yelled desperately, thinking Angelica hadn't heard her. "Before it's too late."

Angelica waved Sophie on with a pale hand and then turned again to face the entrance to Aria's canyon.

That's when Sophie saw him. The mountain lion. He flowed toward Angelica like liquid poison, and even from a distance, Sophie could see the hatred in his eyes. "Angelica!" she shrieked. "Run!"

She watched in horror as the lion closed in on the girl. Then Angelica started to glow. It wasn't a huge burst like before, but a soft, gentle glow. She held her arms out toward the big cat.

And Sophie understood what Angelica was doing. She was acting as bait. She was not only luring the lion away from Aria, Sophie, and Melody, she was luring it into the path of the flood. Stricken, Sophie watched as the lion collected himself, a few yards away from Angelica, preparing to spring.

All Sophie knew as she started to slip off Aria's back was that she had to do something. She didn't know what she could do against such an adversary, but she couldn't leave the older girl to face him alone. But Aria was ready for her. She spun in a circle forcing Sophie to hold onto her mane and grip with her knees.

Suddenly Aria stopped, startled. It took Sophie a second to realize what was wrong. Rumbling filled the canyon. The ground shook and rocks tumbled from the canyon's edge. The flood was coming! Sophie caught a glimpse, a horrible glimpse, of the lion in mid spring. As Aria sped away, Sophie looked back over her shoulder. The cat and Angelica were struggling together, locked in a death grip.

Then the brown wall of water swept around the bend in the canyon, crashed into the far wall, and rolled straight at them. The flood engulfed Angelica and the mountain lion in a heartbeat and bore down on the two horses and the girl, racing for their lives.

"Melody, hurry!" screamed Sophie, looking back to see the young filly struggling behind them. She turned forward again, her eyes locked on the desert that lay before them. Would they make it? No. It was too far. And once on the desert they would still be in the path of the flood. Unless they could get to some elevated ground.

Sophie glanced to her left toward the hills at the canyon mouth. They weren't as steep as the rock walls farther back. Then Sophie remembered a trail that went up one of the hills. Aria seemed to know what Sophie was thinking and angled to the side of the canyon as she ran.

Sophie urged the mare to run faster, bending over her neck and whispering words of encouragement. The brown flood rumbled louder as it came closer. The ground trembled beneath Aria's hooves and Sophie didn't dare look back to see if Melody was okay. Even leaning a bit to one side could throw Aria off her stride and slow her, endangering them all. All she could do was hope the young filly had kept her feet. All she could do was pray that Melody was fast enough.

The water was almost upon them when Aria jumped onto the trail and raced up the incline. Sophie couldn't help herself, she had to look back. She watched horrified as Melody leapt after them. Too late! She was going to be swept away! The raging water grabbed Melody's back legs as she scrambled up the trail and pulled her sideways.

"No! Melody!" Sophie screamed and the filly dug in with her front hooves. She fought with all her might, her new muscles straining with every bit of strength she had. Suddenly she was free. Wide-eyed and winded, the filly raced up the hill to her mother.

At the top, Aria stopped. She nickered through deep breaths and nuzzled Melody, sniffing her all over. Sophie sat on Aria's back, stunned. She looked at the wet filly, then reluctantly her eyes shifted to the brown waters rushing past. From her vantage point, she could see it spread out from the canyon mouth and onto the desert in a dozen smaller streams. Already the force of the water was lessening. Sophie searched for Angelica in the floodwaters, afraid of what she might see, but the muddy tide had swallowed everything. No golden-haired girl struggled on its surface. Or floated face down. Tears blurred Sophie's vision. She couldn't see how Angelica could survive both the flood and the lion's attack. Suddenly a loud neigh pierced the air. *Aria's calling for Angelica,* thought Sophie, but then the mare turned toward the canyon where Sophie had seen the wild horses the night before.

Yesterday, that was only yesterday, thought Sophie, still in shock. *How can so much change in just one day? Oh Angelica, I'm so sorry. It's all my fault. If I hadn't taken Aria away...*

Aria neighed again and began to trot down the far side of the hill, still calling out as she went. Melody hurried behind, still breathing hard.

"Whoa, Aria," said Sophie, coming to her senses. "We have to look for Angelica. We can't just leave."

Aria didn't seem to hear her. As soon as she reached the desert, she broke into a canter. Every few seconds she would send a piercing neigh into the air, calling, searching.

138

And then Sophie heard an answer to the mare's desperate cries. Sky. He was standing on a ridge top in the distance. He neighed once more, then disappeared. Aria stood still and waited.

"What are we doing here, Aria?" asked Sophie. "We have to go back now." She tried to direct the mare back toward the flood with her heels, but Aria wouldn't budge.

"You don't want to live with the wild horses, do you Aria?" Sophie slipped from the mare's back and hugged her neck. "Don't go, Aria," she begged. "Kalene and Joel want you to come home, and I do too. I need to know you're there. Safe. Don't go, Aria, please. We need you."

Aria snorted and nuzzled Sophie and the girl stepped back. After all they had been through Aria and Melody were going to end up with the wild horses.

Sophie felt completely helpless. She knew she wouldn't be able to stop the mare or Melody from leaving. She had no rope. No way to talk to them like Angelica did. And she had no time.

I have to go back to find Angelica, Sophie thought as she turned away. Her hand slid along Melody's back, then she ran toward the flood. *Maybe she's not dead. Maybe I can help her. I have to try.*

She could see the brown flood in the distance quickly growing closer and tried to put Aria and Melody out of her mind as she ran. Only when she heard the hoofbeats did she stop. The entire herd of mustangs was speeding toward the hill she, Aria, and Melody had raced down just minutes before, the lead mare in front with Sky bringing up the rear. And Aria was with them, Melody galloping beside her. The horses trotted up the hill and stood at the top, looking over the floodwaters. Then one of the mares neighed and the herd disappeared over the other side of the hill.

139

Why would they go toward the flood? thought Sophie. *I don't understand. Unless...unless they're going to find Angelica! If they find her, she'll be saved!* Sophie squeezed her eyes shut and lowered her head. *Please God, make her okay! Please help them find her. Please. Please.*

When Sophie finally looked up she saw two horses trotting toward her. Aria and Melody were coming back. Sophie ran to meet the gray mare and the foal. "You found Sky and his herd because you knew they could save Angelica!" she said breathlessly to the mare. "They love her too, and they will cry over her and they will heal her, just like you did, won't they Aria? I'm sorry for not understanding. I'm sorry for thinking you were leaving Angelica behind, that you didn't care about her. I'm sorry for thinking you wanted to go and live with the mustangs." She threw her arms around the mare's neck and buried her face in the silky mane. "I love you so much, Aria," she said in a muffled voice.

She felt Melody's muzzle touch her back and turned. She knelt down and hugged the filly gently around her neck. "I love you too, Melody," she whispered.

Then Aria bumped Sophie with her nose and Sophie looked up to see the mare turn. Slowly, with tired steps, she moved forward. Sophie and Melody followed behind her like two foals. As she walked, Sophie pictured the mustangs standing around Angelica, their heads lowered, their tears splashing like life-giving rain on the fallen girl. And Angelica would rise up. She would be restored. She would carry on to care for more horses and to save more lives. As long as the horses loved her.

I just wish I could have told her goodbye, thought Sophie. *I wish I could have thanked her for everything she did.*

Sophie ruffled Melody's mane as they walked. The filly looked at her with bright eyes and snorted. Sophie smiled

140

and almost opened her mouth to speak. But then she stopped. She didn't have to say anything. Melody understood how she missed Angelica. She could see it in the little filly's eyes.

Darkness. I am alone. . .

And then someone is here. No. Many are here. I can feel them standing around me. The mares and the foals. Willow and Owl. Coyote and Chinook and Cactus and Thunderhead. Snowflake and Tumbleweed and Sparrow. And Sky. They stand around me and their tears fall. They weep because they love me. They weep because I am in pain.

I am so blessed. These gracious ones have honored me with their love. I am full of gratitude at their goodness. I cry too, tears of joy for their amazing beauty.

I, Angelica, am the most fortunate of all beings. I would gladly give everything to serve these beautiful ones. Instead they are the ones who give to me.

Sophie, Aria, and Melody walked slowly across the desert. All of them, especially Melody, were exhausted from their ordeal. Aria stopped once and the filly had a short nap. Sophie lay beside Melody and stroked her soft side as the young horse slept. In fifteen minutes, Aria roused them and, after suckling Melody briefly, they continued on toward the ranch.

It was early afternoon by the time the house came into sight. Sophie took the lead for a moment and the two horses followed her toward the road that ran in front of the house.

Once on the road, Aria's pace quickened. Her head was up and her ears pointed toward home. Melody trotted behind her dam, trying to keep up until she noticed Sophie dragging behind. Then the young filly slowed her steps and walked beside the girl. Sophie put her hand on the filly's back and they walked side by side, both looking apprehensively at the house and barns. Sophie could see Kalene's car in the driveway and realized that Joel must have phoned her when he got home from town and found that Sophie was gone. They would be worried.

When Aria reached the driveway, she didn't hesitate. She turned in and trotted toward her barn. She neighed in greeting to the horses in the paddocks. Halfway down the drive she stopped and looked back at Melody and Sophie just turning off the road. She called Melody to come to her.

Sophie stopped and watched Melody trot to her dam's

side. She wished she could just turn around and run far, far away, now that Melody and Aria were home safe. But then the front door opened and Joel and Kalene come out of the house. It was too late.

Sophie heard the surprise in their voices and watched them hurry to greet Aria. When Aria turned to nuzzle her foal, Kalene and Joel stopped short. Kalene gave a small gasp and Joel let out a low whistle as the filly stood shyly beside her dam. Then, with Melody at her side, Aria walked toward the barn. She wanted to be put into her stall, the one that had stood empty since the day she had left. Melody trotted alongside, leaving Sophie alone to face Joel and Kalene.

But it's better this way, Sophie thought as she stepped forward. *I don't want Melody to hear the anger in their voices. She wouldn't understand and she might be frightened, and she's been frightened too much already.*

Sophie moved slower as she approached Kalene and Joel and finally stopped, her head down. The couple walked the last few steps toward her and Kalene put her hand on Sophie's shoulder. "Tell us what's happening, Sophie," said Kalene.

Sophie didn't know how to start. Silence buzzed around her and she felt dizzy.

"Why don't we all go take care of Aria and her foal," suggested Joel after a moment. "She may want some lunch and the baby looks tired."

"She is," whispered Sophie. Talking about Melody helped her find her voice. "She was only born last night and already she's had to run away from a mountain lion and a flash flood."

"Sophie! Are you okay?" said Kalene. "What happened? And where's your cast?"

144

Sophie glanced up for a second. Joel and Kalene didn't seem too mad yet. "My arm's not broken. See?" she held her arm out for them to look at, bending it a few times to show them. "It must've been a mistake at the hospital. I took the cast off."

"But we saw the X rays," said Kalene and then looked up at Joel. "Maybe they got mixed up with someone else's."

"And what's this about a mountain lion and a flash flood?" asked Joel.

"And that filly," added Kalene. "Where did she come from? She's beautiful." She took a step toward the pair standing at the barn door, pressing her hand on Sophie's shoulder so she would know to come along.

Sophie looked up as she walked, this time with hope in her eyes. "You like her?" she asked.

"She's beautiful. And what an unusual color," said Joel, walking behind them.

Sophie still didn't hear anger in their voices. Or sadness. They actually seemed happy to see Melody. When they reached the two horses, Kalene held her hand out for Melody to sniff. Melody backed up, wary of Kalene. Then she nickered to Sophie and nuzzled her.

"Her name is Melody and her sire is the blue roan mustang stallion," Sophie blurted out. She ran her fingers through Melody's fine hair as she spoke. "I fell asleep last summer and Aria got loose with the wild horses. I thought everything was okay, until…" She stopped. *Just say it,* she commanded herself.

"Until you found out Aria was in foal?" Joel guessed.

"And so you did what, Sophie?" asked Kalene, her voice firm. "Tell us."

Now comes the hard part, thought Sophie as she bent and hugged the filly around the neck. She inhaled the sweet

145

scent of the young horse. It seemed to strengthen her. *Just do it,* she told herself. *Just talk! Tell them and get it over with.*

"I borrowed Aria for a while. I thought you would send me away if you knew I hadn't watched her all the time I was riding her on the desert and would be mad if you knew she was in foal to a wild stallion, even though he's beautiful, so I snuck her away and kept her hidden in one of the canyons," said Sophie, the words coming fast as if another flood had been unleashed. "I was going to keep her there until the foal was born and then weaned and bring her home, saying I found her out on the desert. I was going to turn the foal out with her sire's herd to be a wild horse. But then…" Sophie stopped herself just in time from saying Angelica's name. "But then I was hit by that car and couldn't get out to take care of her and when I finally got there I discovered a mountain lion was hanging around and I knew I had to bring her home. When you asked to adopt me I was so happy and so sad because I knew I still had to tell you the truth, even though you wouldn't want me anymore because you would see what I'm really like. And then this morning when I got to the canyon, Melody was born and then the mountain lion came and while we were running away, the flash flood washed down the canyon behind us and swept the mountain lion away and we almost didn't make it but we did and now I know you probably won't want to adopt me and you might send me away, but I just had to bring Aria and Melody to safety and I was so tired of lying to you. I'm sorry for stealing her away and if I had to do it all over again I would have told you the very first day…"

"Sophie, stop," said Joel, but she didn't hear him. All the countless times she couldn't speak, all the years of silence, were finally over. There was no more holding back. No

146

more being tongue-tied. No more thinking and wishing and trying to get enough courage to say what she dearly wanted to say. She was just *saying* it. A feeling of exhilaration was building inside her and she spoke even faster.

"…and if it wasn't for me nothing bad would've happened to Aria and she wouldn't have been taken from her home and I wish I had told you right away because then you would have sent me away before I got to love you both so much and I wish you could just know how sorry I am but at least if you like Melody that's something, and she will have a happy home and grow up to be a beautiful horse and I'm already going to miss her too and…"

"Sophie!" Kalene and Joel said together, and Sophie finally stopped.

"Sophie," said Joel in a quieter voice. "If you had told us about Aria months ago, we wouldn't have sent you away. You made a mistake, that's all."

"And you never should have taken Aria," said Kalene. "You put her life in danger. And Melody's life too."

"Anything could have happened to her out there. Anything," added Joel.

"But even though you were wrong to take her and you were wrong to not tell us," said Kalene, "we are *not* going to send you away."

"And of course we still want to adopt you," said Joel.

"And you're going to be punished," added Kalene.

Joel nodded and continued. "You're our daughter. Families stick together."

"Remember that next time something happens," said Kalene. "And I hope you can trust us enough to tell us. We've made mistakes too, and we don't expect you to be perfect. But we do expect you to try to always do the right thing and to be the best person you can be."

147

Sophie smiled and her eyes lit up. "You really still want to adopt me?"

"We're your mom and dad, Sport," said Joel. "You're not going to get rid of us that easy."

"Besides, who else can we get to take on a half mustang foal," said Kalene and looked up a Joel.

"That's right," he said, when he realized what Kalene was talking about. "That little filly would be lost without you. What would she think if we sent her owner away?"

"What? You can't mean it, can you?" whooped Sophie, overjoyed. "She's mine?" Then she laughed. "And I'm yours!" she added. She threw one arm around Kalene and the other around Joel. "I can't believe it," she said, her voice muffled by Joel's coat. "I can't believe how lucky I am. Or how wonderful you are!"

"Well now," said Joel, pushing her back. "You wait to decide how wonderful we are. There's work to be done. We've got a couple of horses to take care of, so let's not keep them waiting. And we've got a punishment to work out," he said looking at Kalene.

"Oh yes," said Kalene. "This one will take some thought. I'm glad your arm isn't broken, Sophie. I think we can start in the barn today. All the stalls need mucking out. We'll think of the second phase of the punishment later."

But Sophie was so happy she just nodded her head. A huge grin spread across her face. She couldn't imagine anything more wonderful than shovelling horse manure today, manure from the horses that belonged to her mom and dad.

And from Melody, the little one that belonged to her.

Late that night, Sophie went out to the barn to say good-night to Aria and Melody. It was strange to see them comfortable in their roomy stall instead of the hidden corral. She wondered if Aria and Melody missed the sounds of the desert canyon, the water bubbling from the pool, the wind in the willows, the calls of the night birds.

She scratched Aria under her chin, stroked Melody's neck and whispered, "See you in the morning, Melody," into the foal's ear , then slipped out of the stall and closed the door behind her.

"Sophie." Angelica's voice came from the other end of the barn.

Sophie spun around to see Angelica standing outside Rosie and Starlet's stall. Relief washed over her. "Angelica!" she cried as she ran toward the golden girl. "I'm so glad you are okay! You are, aren't you? The mustangs found you. And what about the mountain lion?"

Angelica smiled. "Yes, I am fine. And the mountain lion was killed." She shook her head and her golden hair shimmered in the light. "He leapt on me just before the flood swept over us. He drowned."

"I'm glad he's dead," said Sophie. "I know I shouldn't be, but I am. And I'm so glad you came to say goodbye."

"I came to give you something too," said Angelica. "And to tell you how happy I am for you and your new parents."

Sophie beamed. "Isn't it wonderful?"

149

"They love you very much," said Angelica. She reached out and touched Sophie's cheek. "And you are worthy of their love."

When Sophie looked down, embarrassed, Angelica continued. "I came to tell you of Starlet too. The Great One wants me to tell you of her, since you will have a part to play in her future."

"I will have something to do with Starlet?" asked Sophie, looking up.

"Yes, she is to become the companion to your best friend. Not now, but in a year or two," said Angelica. "They will have many happy years together, just as you and Melody will."

"You mean Max?" asked Sophie. "That's so weird because Max totally loves Starlet. She has ever since the first time she saw her!"

"You will get the opportunity to bring them together," said Angelica. "When the time is right, you will know what to do, what to say, to make it come to pass."

"I would be happy to help," said Sophie with a smile. Then she grimaced. "I don't suppose I can tell Max, can I?"

Angelica shook her head and smiled.

"That's okay," said Sophie. "She'd never believe me anyway."

Suddenly Angelica gasped and closed her golden eyes. "I can feel someone pulling me…far to the south…a mountain pass…" she whispered. After standing still for another moment her eyes snapped opened. "We must hurry," she said urgently. "Hold out your hand, Sophie."

Angelica put her hand to her hair as her golden tresses began to swirl in a nonexistent wind. Sophie watched her capture a single strand and twine it around her finger. She tugged sharply and placed the hair in Sophie's outstretched palm.

But it was no longer a hair. It was a necklace, as gold-colored as Angelica's locks and as light as air. Sophie touched it with her finger and then lifted it. The necklace tinkled gently and Sophie could feel a soft energy warming her fingers. Sophie leaned forward so Angelica could slip the necklace around her neck. Sophie noticed that Angelica's skin was glowing as she pulled away.

"Thank you," Sophie said breathlessly. She stroked the golden links. "It's the most beautiful necklace I've ever seen."

Angelica glowed brighter. "If you ever need help, Sophie, just touch it with your finger and call my name," she said. "I will hear you and will come."

"Thank you, Angelica," said Sophie. For a second she hesitated, then she stepped forward and threw her arms around the older girl.

Angelica pulled her close for a moment, her arms warm and strong and tingling with energy. Then she pushed Sophie back. "I am sorry, Sophie. I must go," she said. "Gato is calling me. He is in danger."

"Good luck, Angelica," called Sophie. She stepped back as Angelica brightened even more. Each point of her body became as luminous as the heart of a candle and her hair flew around her, not as gold, but as light. Then the form of the girl was gone and Angelica became the swirling brightness. Sophie tried to look at the light, but it hurt too much. With regret, she put her hand over her eyes. She could see the gleam through her fingers and eyelids grow stronger and stronger.

Then it grew less. Slowly, Sophie lowered her hand and opened her eyes. Angelica was gone. Sophie touched the necklace as she stared at the place Angelica had been.

"She sure knows how to make an exit," she said to the barnfull of horses.

Melody and Starlet neighed in agreement.

152

Gato. You are in grave peril.

And your companion, the lovely Fresa, has fallen. I am too late to save her. Too late. My heart weeps with great pain and sorrow.

But I will not be too late to save you, Gato. I must save you from the same fate that befell Fresa, for the condors will soon return.